Bettie Sutton

Jack strode to his truck, leaving Kristi puzzled and staring after him.

At times his peculiar behavior caused her to want to shake him. Other moments, like these, she could only label him as a hurting man who desperately needed Jesus. The mention of his family changed him from congenial to distant. It seemed he couldn't get away fast enough.

So there must lie the problem. A family squabble, she surmised. How could families treat each other so shamefully? A twinge of guilt settled over her. She knew exactly how loved ones could hurt others.

No matter what the root of Jack's melancholia, he needed to reconcile with God before he could ever take a step toward happiness.

She sat in the gazebo long after the stars studded a cloudless, navy sky, listening to the dulcimer hymns coming from the speakers above her head. In the quietness of night with the hum of singing insects raising their voices, Kristi prayed for guidance and direction.

W9-BYN-993

DIANN MILLS lives in Houston, Texas, with her husband Dean. They have four adult sons. She wrote from the time she could hold a pencil, but not seriously until God made it clear that she should write for Him. After three years of serious writing, her first book *Rehoboth* won favorite **Heartsong Presents** historical for 1998. Other publishing credits include magazine articles and short stories, devotionals, poetry, and internal writing for her church. She is an active church choir member, leads a ladies' Bible study, and is a church librarian.

Books by DiAnn Mills

Don't miss out on any of our super romances. Write to us at the following address for information on our newest releases and club information.

Heartsong Presents Readers' Service
PO Box 719
Uhrichsville, OH 44683

Equestrian Charm

DiAnn Mills

Heartsong Presents

Many are the plans in a man's heart, but it is the LORD's purpose that prevails. Proverbs 19:21

To Rhita McNair. Thank you for all of your wonderful help in researching Arabian horses.

A note from the author:
I love to hear from my readers! You may correspond with me by writing: **DiAnn Mills**
                                        Author Relations
                                        PO Box 719
                                        Uhrichsville, OH 44683

ISBN 1-58660-021-4

EQUESTRIAN CHARM

Scripture taken from the HOLY BIBLE: NEW INTERNATIONAL VERSION®. NIV®. Copyright© 1973, 1978, 1984 by International Bible Society. Used by permission of Zondervan Publishing House.

© 2000 by Barbour Publishing, Inc. All rights reserved. Except for use in any review, the reproduction or utilization of this work in whole or in part in any form by any electronic, mechanical, or other means, now known or hereafter invented, is forbidden without the permission of the publisher, Heartsong Presents, PO Box 719, Uhrichsville, Ohio 44683.

All of the characters and events in this book are fictitious. Any resemblance to actual persons, living or dead, or to actual events is purely coincidental.

Cover design by Jocelyne Bouchard.

PRINTED IN THE U.S.A.

one

Kristi Franklin's heels slowly clicked along the pavement until a quick glimpse at her watch spurred her steps. Anchoring the straps of her shoulder bag in place, she fixed her gaze on the Banner Press and raced toward the newspaper office with less than five minutes to spare.

Perspiration beaded upon her forehead in the ninety-degree heat and high humidity. Dampness formed on her back and moistened her silk blouse and jacket. *Why didn't I take care of this yesterday?* she inwardly moaned. *Then I wouldn't be running in this heat after spending the day inside an air-conditioned office.*

Kristi's hand grasped the doorknob at the same time a car alarm pierced the air. The sound jarred her nerves as though it summoned the five o'clock hour. Flinging open the door, she plunged into her spiel.

"Sorry to barge in right at closing, but I need to stop an ad before tomorrow's paper. Dad sold his ranch and doesn't need to advertise it in the next edition. Anyway, I was supposed to take care of this yesterday, but I forgot, which is why I'm here at five o'clock." She caught her breath and sighed.

A chubby middle-aged woman with carrot-colored hair lifted an eyebrow. "Honey, do you think you could repeat that in ten seconds or less?"

Kristi felt herself smile, then break into laughter. "Probably not. Am I too late, Norma?"

"Absolutely," Norma replied, removing her turquoise-rimmed glasses attached to a gold chain around her neck. "But for you, we'll make an exception."

5

"You're a sweetheart," Kristi replied and leaned onto the counter separating them, reveling in the cool temperature. "And you will keep me out of hot water with Dad."

"Hey, Kristi!" A balding fellow greeted her from behind a corner desk. "Who bought the place?"

Kristi cringed and nibbled on her lower lip. "I can't remember his name, but he raises Arabian horses."

"You've got news, girl—front page news for the *Banner*. Impossible to turn you into a reporter when you can't recall names."

Kristi grinned. "I'll try harder, Chip."

"Don't you flash those big brown eyes at me," he teased. "My poor old heart can't take it."

"Umph," Norma scolded with a toss of her shoulder-length hair. "Why don't you just pull Rick's ad and leave her alone."

Chip jutted out his chin in mock annoyance. "Sure, yes ma'am, anything for my beloved wife."

Norma blew him a kiss and turned her attention to Kristi. "Pretty green suit. Did you have a seminar today?"

"Yes, Brenham National had me do an investment workshop for its employees."

The older woman's blue eyes sparkled. "Isn't the vice president there single?"

"I wouldn't know." Kristi frowned. "I'm not in the market for a husband, remember?"

"Oh, that's what you keep telling everyone, but I don't believe it for a minute." Norma tilted her head and nodded to emphasize her words. "Someday, some man is going to sweep you off your feet and land you at the altar repeating 'I do.' "

"Not me," she replied. "I am a career woman, and you can quote me on that one."

"It'll be in the next edition," Chip called. "Kristi Franklin once again states she's a career woman."

Kristi laughed. "Perfect, now all I have to do is convince

you two, my parents, and half of Brenham." She took a passing glance at her watch. "Oops, I really need to get going. Told Mom I'd be home by five-thirty." She waved good-bye and left the newspaper office for her candy-apple red convertible parked a block down Stringer Drive.

As soon as Kristi reached her car, she heard someone call her name. Looking up, she saw her stepfather pull his bronze Explorer alongside her.

"Hey, lady, heading home?" he greeted.

Kristi peered into the lowered passenger's window at the silver-haired gentleman she lovingly called Dad. "Yes, what about you?"

"Oh, I've got an appointment with a client in Elgin. It'll be late before I'm finished. Say, could I get you to do me a big favor?"

"Sure."

He produced a set of keys from the console. "I forgot to give Jack the extra set of keys to the ranch. Would you mind dropping them off?"

"Can do," she replied. *Now I remember the new owner's name—Jack Frazier.*

"And," he continued, pointing to a camera perched on the seat, "I picked this up a few minutes ago. It's loaded and ready for you to snap away."

Kristi gladly offered her best smile and opened the passenger door to retrieve her camera. "Thanks. Maybe I can get in some shots this evening."

Her dad chuckled. "Did you get the ad cancelled before the paper closed?"

Kristi nodded. Caught. "Yes, sir, I did. Were you watching me race to their office?"

"Yes. And a mighty fine sight you made, too," he added, his crystal blue eyes dancing. "Although I wondered if you planned to break both legs in those heels."

Giving him a smug look while he enjoyed another laugh, Kristi snatched up the camera. "Whoever did you tease before I came along?"

"No one," he replied. "You bring out the best in me."

A car tooted behind them causing Kristi to shut the door and wave as he sped down the street. Entering her own car, she started the engine and pulled away from the curb while punching in the number to her parents' bed and breakfast.

"Good afternoon, Country Charm," a familiar voice answered.

Kristi heard the warmth in her mother's voice. She envisioned her tall, attractive mom fussing with her auburn hair as though the caller could see her, a habit that caused a mound of teasing. "Hi, Mom, I'll be home in about thirty minutes or so. Dad asked me to drop off some keys at the ranch."

"Okay, I've started dinner. How about chicken Alfredo, a salad, and hot herb bread?"

"Thought I smelled something heavenly. I'll let my nose drive me home. Looks like another night of running five miles after I've eaten," Kristi moaned. She turned a corner onto a main highway. "How many guests tonight?"

"Two couples and an elderly woman from Austin. All have checked in and won't be back until later."

"Do you need anything from the store?"

"Hmm. . .no, but thanks."

A moment later, Kristi replaced the cell phone. Tonight she must bring up the subject of her own apartment. She'd lived with her parents for the past year and a half since a near fatal car accident rendered her completely helpless. It took more than six months to fully recover the shattered parts of her life— broken bones, a broken line of communication with her mother, and a broken relationship with the Lord. All were her fault.

After her father had died several years before, Kristi had allowed self-pity and self-indulgence to nearly destroy her. She'd climbed the corporate ladder in a large investment firm, convinced that power and money would satisfy the yearning in her soul. If those things weren't enough, when her mother decided to open a Christian bed and breakfast, Kristi took her to court in an effort to prove her incompetent. Her mother's friendship with Rick Davenport, a local building contractor in Brenham, Texas, infuriated Kristi even more. At the time, she felt certain she could handle her mother's inheritance in a much better way than sinking it into a remodeling venture, plus she suspected Rick was vying for her mother's money. Kristi had been so far from the truth.

Fortunately, the judge foiled Kristi's plans, but then bitterness took more of a foothold in her life. Just before her mother and Rick married, Kristi drove her car into a concrete embankment. She'd wanted to die—too tired of life and its misery. Through Rick's patience and persistence, she finally experienced the wonder of God's love. The couple married, and now the three shared the joy of a close-knit family.

In the beginning, Kristi didn't know what to call her stepfather. After much prayer and deliberation, she asked his permission to call him Dad. He had other children in the area, and she didn't know how he or they would feel about it. She remembered the tears in his eyes. He said nothing but simply drew her and her mother into a big bear hug.

Her mom and dad's hard work certainly paid off because the bed and breakfast, appropriately named Country Charm, remained full with a waiting list. It not only offered the typical amenities bathed in hospitality and excellent food, but lavish decorating with matchless antiques, an extensive library, hayrides in the evening, a farm animal petting area, and a stocked pond for fishing—all wrapped in a Christian theme.

Once her body mended, Kristi helped with the bed and breakfast and worked part time as an investment consultant giving seminars from Austin to Houston. Her assistance with Country Charm allowed her parents to occasionally get away for a few days, and she planned to continue regardless of where she lived. But lately Kristi sensed a deep need to be on her own again. Her independent nature spurned the thought of taking advantage of those nearest and dearest to her heart although every time she suggested the weaning, her parents refused to hear of it. Kristi had to smile. Was she sixteen or twenty-six?

She turned left on the country road leading to the ranch once belonging to her stepdad. Recently he had transported five quarter horse mares to the Country Charm and sold the rest. Kristi knew he hated parting with them. Her dad simply didn't have time between the bed and breakfast and supervising his contracting company to properly care for the animals.

Kristi parked in the circular driveway and exited her car to ring the doorbell of the stately Victorian home. A few moments later, she realized Mr. Jack Frazier was not available. Curiosity tugged at her. She really wanted to see those Arabian horses, especially since she knew nothing about that particular breed. Locking her convertible, she snatched up her camera and headed toward the stables and pasture.

Photography had aroused her interest last fall when a professional from a national magazine arrived to take pictures of the bed and breakfast. It looked fun, and the more she observed, the more she desired to learn what the photographer saw through the camera's lens. What started out as a passing fancy quickly turned into a hobby.

Standing in the late afternoon heat, Kristi knew she couldn't leave until she snapped a few pictures of Jack Frazier's Arabian horses.

"Hello," she called, rounding the house, armed with her camera.

Satisfied no one observed her, Kristi observed several horses in the pasture. They weren't a particular color—brown to gray, but they held a magnificent, regal stance. Their faces were shaped differently from other horses, more of a triangle. She tiptoed closer to the fence and removed her shoes so her heels wouldn't sink into the soft earth. Setting them aside, she noted more of the Arabians' unique features—long, thin nostrils and large, wide-set eyes. Suddenly the image of an Egyptian sheik riding across the desert entertained her thoughts.

"Wow," she whispered and studied a beautiful chestnut stallion. Kristi raised the camera and aimed while excitement surged through her veins. She snapped a second, third, and fourth picture.

"Hey, what are you doing?" someone shouted in a New York accent.

Kristi jumped and whirled around to see a man heading her way, none too happy and definitely not a swarthy looking chieftain.

"I'm taking pictures of these horses—"

"I'm no idiot. I can see what you're doing," he snapped. He ran his fingers through straw-colored hair and glared at her. "Now what are you doing here?"

Oh, great, she thought. *I sure hope this fellow doesn't work for the new owner.* "I'm looking for Mr. Frazier."

"Why?" he bellowed.

"I don't think that's any of your business," she said with an air of sophistication, lifting her chin to defy him. Kristi didn't like this man's attitude at all. Luckily she stood eye level with him without her shoes which made him appear less intimidating.

His slate gray gaze narrowed. "Are you a newspaper reporter?"

"No!"

"Then why are you taking pictures?"

Kristi swallowed an angry retort. "It's a hobby. Do you have a problem with special interests?"

"Yeah, when it involves my horses."

Silence captured the moments between them while tension split the air.

"You're Jack Frazier?" she asked, hoping she'd heard wrong.

"Do you want to see my driver's license?"

Cocky, rude, and smart-mouthed, she thought. *What a wonderful person to have purchased Dad's ranch, and a pillar of personality to match.* "Well, if my Dad had informed me the new owner lacked manners, maybe I would have been prepared."

"You're Rick Davenport's daughter?" His accent was laced with disbelief. "But I thought you were—"

"I know what you thought," she said and stomped off toward her car, her arms swinging with exasperation and the weight of her camera. Drawing in her breath, she turned and managed to stop the tonnage of livid words seeking to grace her lips. "Your keys, Mr. Frazier, will be on the driveway in front of your house." She lifted her shoulders and made her way to the car, painfully aware that she'd left her shoes behind.

With immense pleasure, she tossed the keys in front of the front door and drove off, already regretting her unchristian display of anger but too irate to do a thing about it.

two

By the time Kristi steered her sports car into the oversized driveway of her home, she shook with indignation. A thousand ways of getting even with Jack Frazier danced across her mind.

"Calm yourself," she said, flipping the air conditioning to near freezing. The old Kristi and her infamous temper threatened to take over any resemblance of "love thy neighbor," except she never expected those commands to encompass Mr. Frazier. How could one Yankee be so unfriendly?

She glanced up at the converted one-hundred-year-old farmhouse. Her gaze swept over the manicured lawn adorned in bold summer colors and a huge, sprawling live oak holding up its green branches to a cloudless sky. The Country Charm sign swayed slightly in the breeze, and the verse painted on it captured her attention: "Come with me by yourselves to a quiet place and get some rest"—Mark 6:31.

Okay, Lord, I get the message. I did a lousy job of mirroring Jesus, and Jack Frazier's rudeness is no excuse. Revenge is not mine to give, contemplate, or dwell upon. I'm sorry, and I promise the next time I see him, I'll be nice.

Harry, her mother's collie, loped up to the car, wagging his tail furiously and begging for her to exit. His soft brown eyes seemed to coax a smile from her, and she relinquished. Her mother often said God gave pets for man to see the value of kindness. Another lesson dutifully applied to her recent encounter with Mr. Unfriendly.

Walking toward the back door and listening to the faint dulcimer sounds of "Amazing Grace" floating through the outside speakers of the gazebo eased her spirit. Although Kristi knew she needed to live on her own, the sweet fragrance of home sure could soothe a woman's fragile nerves.

ها

Her mother reached for a box of tissues to dab her moistened eyes. Still laughing, she caught her breath and peered into Kristi's flushed face.

"Mom, I don't see what is so funny," Kristi said, fighting the urge to break into mirth along with her mother. Suddenly, it all did seem funny. She pictured herself stomping across the driveway, too proud to wince when the tiny stones jabbed into her feet.

"I know the man needs a lesson in manners, but think about it, Kris. The whole thing reminds me of two bantam roosters going at each other. And your shoes. . ." Her mother burst into laughter again, and this time Kristi joined her.

"Yeah, and I paid a good price for them, too—designer heels," she said, silently admitting more remorse for the loss of shoes than her unkempt temper.

"So, are you going back for them?"

"Ouch." Kristi cringed. "I'd like to say 'over my dead body,' but my behavior didn't earn any awards, either." She opened a cabinet door and took out a glass. "Guess I could drive back over there and apologize, find my shoes, and then invite him to church."

Her mother chuckled. "What a testimony. I'll have to pass this one on to the pastor. Sounds like a great object lesson to me."

Kristi poured a glass of lemonade from the refrigerator and allowed the sugary drink to sweeten her disposition. "You, of all people, should know the extent of my humility." She stared at her mother for a long moment, reflecting on the scene at her dad's former ranch. "All right. I'll change clothes and head back that way. Will dinner wait?"

"Of course. . .and Kristi?"

"Yeah, Mom."

"This time wear tennis shoes and tie them tightly in double knots like I used to do when you were a little girl."

In feigned annoyance, she rolled her eyes. "You and Dad must spend all of your time conjuring up ways to tease me."

A few minutes later, Kristi emerged from her bedroom in jogging shorts, a tank top, and tennis shoes.

"Okay, I'm leaving as soon as I stop by the barn," she said, pulling her hair through a ponytail holder.

Her mother gazed at her curiously through large hazel eyes.

"A harness for my mouth."

They shared another chuckle and hugged each other before Kristi wrapped her fingers around her keys and hurried outside. She chose to take Harry along for company, or maybe she needed the dog to boost her morale. In any event, she lowered the top on her convertible and drove toward Jack Frazier's ranch.

Relishing the wind cooling her face, Kristi attempted to verbalize her apology with Harry as a captive audience. To her satisfaction, the dog gave no response. The Victorian house came into view, and she began to regret her decision. Even her expensive shoes weren't worth the inner turmoil of admitting a mistake. Maybe he wouldn't be around.

"Dear Lord," she said, and Harry gave her his complete attention. She patted the collie's sleek fur. "Not you, Harry, God. Help me do the right thing here because by myself, I'll lose my temper again."

Braking her car in the circular driveway beside the home, Kristi instructed Harry to stay inside. Taking a deep breath, she turned off the engine, still sorting her jumbled words when she knew she should be relying on God. As she had less than an hour before, Kristi rang the doorbell. Again, no one answered.

Glancing back at Harry, she felt relief wash over her like

the shower she so desperately needed. *Well, Lord, I tried, but he isn't at home. I'll call later or stop by tomorrow.* With a spring in her step, Kristi walked back to the car.

"Did you forget something?" a voice asked in a New York accent.

She glanced in the direction of the stables to see the new owner ambling her way. From this distance, he looked like a kid—a slight frame and a tousle of light-colored hair. If the situation hadn't been so uncomfortable, she might have laughed. There he strode, one hand shoved into his jeans pocket and the other dangling her three-inch heels.

Here, I go, Lord, she thought and met Jack midway on the pavement. His face glistened in the late afternoon heat. Obviously he wasn't accustomed to the soaring Texas temperatures. Kristi extended her hand in hopes the man understood a gesture of friendship.

"I think I need to start all over again," she said, feeling determined. "I'm Kristi Franklin."

He pulled his right hand from his pocket and brushed her fingers with a loose shake. "Jack Frazier." He nodded while eyeing her with a raised brow. "I thought you were Rick Davenport's daughter."

Now I know what the expression means—cold Yankee, she realized. He looked rather emotionless from her point of view. No personality. "He's my stepfather."

"Oh, I see. Uh, here are your shoes," he said, and his gray eyes seemed a little less slate-like and a little more human.

"Thank you."

"About before, I acted rather presumptuously," he continued, and Kristi tried not to smile at the foreign sound of his words. "I thought you were a reporter, and I don't care for them."

She held her shoes in front of her, mentally phrasing her fast approaching apology. Unfortunately, Kristi remembered the days when she would have sliced him up in one seething glare and a spillage of condescending quips. The memories set like pound cake after a heavy dinner.

Being from the North had nothing to do with rudeness; she'd already proved that unfair assessment by reflecting upon her past behavior.

"I suppose I did resemble a member of the press with my camera and all. Mr. Frazier, I am sorry for losing my temper. Around here, we take great pride in being hospitable, and I hope you don't judge everyone in Brenham by my bad manners. It never occurred to me to ask permission before photographing your horses." She took another breath. "So, will you forgive me for not welcoming you properly into the community and not respecting your private property?"

The hint of a smile tugged at his mouth, and she detected milky white teeth beneath his thin lips. "Of course, Miss Franklin. And," he coughed, "I've been edgy with the recent move, a lot on my mind. Didn't know what to expect from the people around here. I'm not from the South. . .New York, in fact."

"I detected your accent." Kristi relaxed and felt a wave of amiability. The way he said New Yawk, rather amused her. *Thank You, Lord. Sorry I'm so hardheaded.* "I imagine a relocation across the country would be a difficult adjustment. Southerners, as a rule, are supposed to be friendly, and I hope you give me an opportunity to make a better impression."

Jack stiffened. "I'm not much of an extrovert—stay to myself. I seem to get along best with horses."

Ignoring his admission, she glanced beyond him to the pasture. "They are beautiful animals. Rather magnificent."

He turned to follow her gaze. "Arabians are my lifeblood," he murmured.

When an uneasy silence passed between them, Kristi decided she needed to return home. "I must be going," she announced. "Good luck with Dad's ranch, and do stop by our bed and breakfast. It's right down the road, and we would love to have you visit." She started to walk away, stopped, and whirled back around. "If you're looking for a church home, we'd be glad to have you attend ours."

Jack studied her with an odd look upon his face, which showed rather nice looking features—tanned and rugged. She wondered if he had been a jockey with his small, lean build. Perhaps he looked at her strangely because of her Southern accent. The uptown jargon of the hi-tech business world had been replaced by country simplicity, and certainly her Texas drawl had deepened during the last eighteen months.

"Do I talk strangely to you?" she asked curiously.

He wet his lips. "Unfamiliar best describes it. It's going to take some getting used to on my part."

"I understand." She paused. "Well, have a pleasant evening, and thanks for not tossing my shoes."

Once seated in her car, Kristi opened her console and rewarded Harry with a doggy-treat for good behavior. She stared out at Jack leaning against the fence with his back to her. Soon, two Arabians paraded in front of him. Maybe he did fare better with horses than people. After further deliberation about their conversation, she thought his aloofness and crusty shell masked something else, perhaps loneliness. Strange, he didn't reply to her invitation to church.

Laughing lightly, Kristi stuck her key into the ignition. She'd been filling her late hours with far too many classic movies and mystery novels.

❧

Jack rubbed the faint star marking on the head of his favorite chestnut stallion, Desert Wind. What an excellent representation of his commitment to the Arabian breed. With a deep sense of pride, he patted the horse's neck and once more appreciated the animal's superior intelligence, enduring strength, and keen devotion not evident in other lines. Fortunately, his horses adapted quickly to the Texas environment, far different from the weather and climate of upstate New York. At Kingston Hills, he had two thousand acres of lush pastureland, but here his fifteen hundred acres would starve a horse in knee-deep grass. He'd spent a fortune in supplementing their diet with sweet oats and hay.

As of yet, he hadn't named the farm, or rather ranch, as Rick Davenport called it. He needed to come up with a title—couldn't print stationery or cards without it.

The sound of Kristi Franklin's red convertible starting up and speeding down the road broke his musings, but he refused to acknowledge her leaving. The days of encouraging friendships had vanished months before; he'd learned his lesson the hard way. Business relationships were vital to his livelihood, but nothing else. He'd been forced from one state, and unless a snooping reporter ruined it for him, Brenham would be his home.

The stallion elected to dart across the pasture in the typical Arabian fashion, his head and tail held high. What a tremendous picture his unique carriage cast against an approaching sunset. Jack loved his horses; everything about them excited and intrigued him.

Unwanted thoughts of Kristi Franklin crept into his mind. Rick Davenport's description of her didn't match the woman. A master's degree in finance and expertise in the business world led Jack to believe she'd be refined, not, he chuckled, full of fire.

At their first meeting, Kristi's beauty nearly took his breath away, most noticeably those huge, mink-colored eyes and full, dark lips. One look and he saw danger. She had no idea of the way he intended to lash out at her before she turned around. All those tales of Southern belles suddenly held credibility, complete in a delightful blend of drawn-out vowels and no shoes. Even her temper and spunk appealed to him. A lonely man needed to steer free of a woman who represented those things he desperately craved.

Odd, she returned to apologize when he had set the tone for bad manners. A twinge of remorse stung him like the sunburn plaguing his arms. His treatment of her would have appalled him in the past. The brusque responses disgusted him, but self-preservation ruled his mind and heart.

Sighing deeply, he recalled the helpfulness of the people he'd encountered in Brenham, in defiance of his resolve to keep everyone at bay. Jack shrugged. With his dour personality, he hoped the stable hands stayed on. This morning he'd treated a young Latino man and his cousin contemptuously for their expert advice on training. They'd come highly recommended from Rick Davenport as dependable and knowledgeable. Guilt caused him to shake his head in an effort to dispel unpleasant memories. The old Jack respected the input of all who shared in his pledge for excellence. He yearned to dive in and be a part of a great part of the country, get involved with good people, and possibly one day find a church home. Impossible.

All the while he pondered over his new surroundings, Jack wondered if he'd ever get used to Southern living.

three

Three weeks passed, and Kristi immersed her energies into financial planning and investing seminars from Brenham to Austin. The stock brokerage firm in Austin where she once enjoyed a prominent position offered her a job, but she refused. After the car accident nearly two years ago and establishing the Lord in her life, she'd resigned with no thought of ever returning. None of the executives understood the loss of high dollars and power, and she doubted if any of them comprehended it now. Although Kristi did attempt to convey the gospel to her former peers, her convictions met with ridicule and criticism. She didn't mind stepping into big business arena as a part of her job, but her heart dwelled in the country.

A deep need to draw closer to her mother and stepfather and help others in a less demanding atmosphere dominated her life. Happy and content best described Kristi, and she intended to stay that way.

The bed and breakfast whirled with activity, seeped in the continuous flow of guests. In addition, various organizations and families booked company picnics and reunions on the grounds. She loved submerging herself in people—making sure they were comfortable at Country Charm and leading tours of the property when her parents were busy.

As in the past, the mention of acquiring an apartment in Brenham met with objections, but Kristi persisted. Her mother and dad wanted her at home as their little girl. Naturally, they denied that conclusion. Kristi loved them dearly, but a grown woman needed a home of her own.

In Kristi's search, she marveled at the changes in her tastes. In Austin she owned a condo, expensively decorated in sleek contemporary furnishings. Now she considered a remodeled duplex built in the thirties. Instead of chrome and glass, she wanted the flavor of yesterday—lots of wood and room for choice antiques.

On those rare occasions when she allowed her reflections to wander, she wondered if Jack had settled into his new home. He'd become somewhat of an enigma to her, especially when her dad said Jack had owned and operated one of the largest Arabian horse farms in the country. Why did he leave a successful operation in New York for small town Texas? When Kristi expressed interest in his background, her dad shrugged his shoulders. "He asked me to keep his private life confidential."

"I see," she replied, remembering Jack's reaction to her trespassing on his property. "He must prefer to keep to himself."

"Yeah, sweetie. Pray for him, will you? I believe he needs good friends and the Lord."

A ton of questions bombarded her, but she respected her dad too much to press him. He visited Jack a few times to encourage him to attend church, but nothing resulted. Her mother left countless messages on his answering machine inviting him to dinner; he didn't return her calls.

One Saturday afternoon, Kristi curled up in a high back, green velvet chair in the parlor of Country Charm and perused a real estate magazine. Failing to hear her dad enter the room, she startled at his voice.

"Are you hiding out?" he asked, bending to give her a kiss on the forehead. "I've been looking everywhere for you."

Kristi closed the magazine and laid it aside. "What do you need?"

"Don't look so innocent," he accused, his crystal blue eyes twinkling. "I see the real estate magazine in your hand." He combed his fingers through thick, silver hair. "You have a home, sweetheart."

"Not mine," she corrected with a smile and a wag of her finger. "But we've gone over this before."

"True," he said with a sigh. "No point arguing with the women in this household. I always lose."

She grinned. "I love you."

"Uh-huh," he replied. "Those words work with your mother, too."

Reaching up to take his hand, she gave it a gentle squeeze. "I love this house and being with you and Mom, but I need my own home," Kristi murmured.

Smiling, he handed her a copy of *American Horseman* magazine. "I really do understand." He paused before continuing. "I found a contest for amateur photographers." His announcement held her spellbound. "Thought it might interest you."

"Oh, it does," she whispered, scanning the article before her. "A perfect opportunity to use my new camera, and," she wiggled her shoulders, "your horses will make excellent subjects."

"Well," her dad drawled. "I was thinking more on the lines of Arabian horses."

Kristi glanced up. "Dad, Jack Frazier doesn't want anyone photographing his horses, remember?"

"Especially when they leave their shoes behind?" He chuckled. "But then you didn't ask permission. He may feel differently, now."

Scrunching her nose, she flashed a questioning look. "Do you have something up your sleeve?"

"Maybe."

Kristi shook her head. "Dad, you're not matchmaking again, are you?"

"Absolutely not," he declared. "I saw the contest, considered the competition. . .and looked at the first prize." He pointed to the article. "A week's paid vacation at a dude ranch in Montana. What do you think?"

"I really don't know," she began, "but I'll think about it. A dude ranch sounds more like your and Mom's kind of a trip." She nibbled on her lower lip. "Seriously, I don't think Jack cares for me."

"Why don't you go over there with me this afternoon? He's supposed to show me around and explain the business."

She considered the request. Granted, she hadn't planned a single thing for the afternoon, and the contest intrigued her. "All right," she agreed slowly. "But if he acts like I'm a pest, I won't bother asking him about taking pictures of his horses."

After lunch, Kristi accompanied her dad in his bronze Explorer to the horse ranch. She didn't feel the same excitement evident in her dad's demeanor, but curiosity held her interest.

ϑ

Ambivalent feelings plagued Jack while he arranged the last of his prized framed photographs on a paneled wall. He'd worked all morning on his newly constructed office in the main barn—filing papers and working on a display wall. At first he wanted only those pictures of his Arabians, but later he decided to add a few of himself dressed in Egyptian attire and mounted on Desert Wind. On his oak desk lay two photographs of War King, a black stallion used by a movie company in Hollywood. With a sigh, he turned over the memories. Those were the good old days, and he regretted parting with War King to pay court costs. Of course, selling the stallion only started his list of disappointments.

With a heavy sigh, he spotted the many boxes filled with dated horse magazines piled in a corner. He should have discarded a lot of them before he moved, but he couldn't bring himself to part with the information.

From outside his office, the sound of a Christian radio station blared in his ears. The trainers played it regularly, and today it irritated him.

"When the misery of today stumbles into your lonely heart
"God is there beside you, His mercy to impart.
"His shoulders are big enough to shelter the heaviest load
"And His love will—"

Jack trudged down the office hallway and slammed the door shut. The last thing he wanted to hear was another song about God's mercies. What a parody. God dangled man on a puppet string for His own amusement, teasing, taunting, and tormenting him until the day he died. "Glad I wised up," he told himself.

When his stomach growled, Jack grabbed a ham sandwich he'd made an hour earlier. A half-eaten bag of sour cream and onion potato chips washed down with bottled water had failed to fill the empty hole. Taking a huge bite, he checked the time. Rick Davenport said he'd stop by after lunch for a personal tour.

With a labored breath, his gaze scanned the office. It looked presentable, although the room would look better once the new sofa and chair arrived. He'd left his old furniture at Kingston Hills, including family portraits. No point in being reminded of the past any more than necessary.

While Jack chewed on his sandwich, he mentally calculated how long before he turned a profit. Lawyers hounded him for payment, and he despised owing money. . .or favors.

A knock at the door interrupted his thoughts. Must be Rick. Jack hoped the former owner didn't plan to use this afternoon as an excuse to talk about God again. He'd heard enough, and Rick Davenport knew the truth about Kingston Hills.

Pasting a smile upon his face and mustering the courage to face the man, Jack opened the door. He expected to see the previous owner but not his stepdaughter. The sight of Kristi snatched his breath away, and it took a moment for him to regain his composure.

" 'Afternoon, Jack," Rick greeted with a wide grin and extended his hand for a hearty shake. "Hope you don't mind me bringing Kristi along."

"No, of course not," Jack replied, grasping the hand. "Hi, Kristi. Glad you came." Holding on to his office door, he wondered where his welcome for Rick's stepdaughter originated.

"Thanks. It's good to see you," she warmly replied.

He felt her warm mink gaze pierce through the barred citadels of his heart. It angered him, for he'd forbidden those emotions to ever rise again.

Kristi smiled. "What I've seen so far around here is impressive."

"I'm glad you like it," Jack said, avoiding eye contact. He motioned for the two to come inside. "There are a couple of chairs across from my desk. We can start here in my air-conditioned office, talk about what is involved in raising Arabians, then move outside. Unlike you, I'm having to adjust to these hot temperatures."

Rick chuckled. "Oh, there are days when we don't handle 'em very well, either."

Jack watched Kristi proceed down the hallway, her slender figure wrapped nicely in faded jeans and a pale yellow, sleeveless top. Like the last time he saw her, she wore her cocoa brown hair in a high ponytail, obviously a cooler option.

"Um, smells heavenly," she said with an appreciative glance. "I love the fresh smell of wood."

"Definitely more appealing than the stalls," Jack said, remembering his resolve to keep these people at a distance. "But I'm more on the same wavelength with horses."

Rick pointed to the display wall. "These are great pictures." Glancing about him at the transformation of what once was a corner of his barn, he continued. "Why didn't I ever think of this?"

"Because your life is immersed in construction and a bed

and breakfast," Kristi pointed out, peering at a photograph of a black stallion.

Rick nodded, still studying the horse-and-rider pictures. "Point well taken, Kristi. Jack, have you chosen a name for your operation yet?"

He ran his fingers through his hair. "Yeah, I've decided on Bedouin Stables."

"Excellent," Rick said. "My knowledge of Arabians is limited, and I've been looking forward to this. Who knows, I may need to add one of your horses to my stables."

"Anytime," Jack said and dived into his favorite subject, explaining how the Arabians were originally used by the Bedouin people and revered for their incredible endurance in the desert.

"So the Arabian is basically a show horse, bred to keep the line pure?" Kristi asked, her interest evident in the way she leaned closer to listen.

"Well, they're a favorite for pleasure riding, too."

"Okay," Rick began. "Tell me why I would want an Arabian."

Jack smiled. "So you want to purchase one today?"

"Don't press him," Kristi warned, her dark eyes sparkling, "or he'll be riding one back home. But I'd like to know the answer."

Jack eased back in his chair. Finally he could relax. Rick and Kristi were attentive, and for the first time in months, he was enjoying himself. "Everyone who appreciates fine horses has a preference. I value the Arabians' superior intelligence and unequaled devotion. Of course I'm biased." He laughed. "They are a breed that attracts men, women, and children. To be honest, they can be taught just about anything—depends on what you want. I have a friend in Virginia who likes to see how many tasks he can teach a horse."

"All right, show me around," Rick announced, rising to his

feet. "Good thing I left my checkbook at home."

Kristi, Rick, and Jack moved from the cool office to the barn. Some of the forty horses stabled there belonged to famous people who allowed Bedouin Stables to care for and train their prized animals.

"When I moved my operation, many of my clients chose to have their horses transported here so I could continue my work with them," he said. Jack felt elation surge through his veins, a pleasant remembrance of the glory days at Kingston Hills. There, he'd spend five hours showing horses to a prospective buyer, then treat the potential client to an elaborate lunch on the grounds.

With the present joy of displaying his horses, an inkling of hope for the future temporarily chased away the black depression often plaguing him.

Jack bridled and led a gray mare out for them to see. "This is Rosie, one of my gentlest mares. In New York, I used her as a lesson horse."

Kristi's eyes widened. "So you plan to give riding lessons?"

"No," he replied, more sternly than he intended. He cringed as an awkward silence passed among them. "I'm sorry, didn't mean to cut you short. Giving lessons can be a real headache."

Rick leaned against Rosie's stall and gave Jack a reassuring smile. "I can imagine," he said, reaching out to pat the mare. "You've probably seen enough spoiled kids and unteachable adults. I wouldn't want the job."

His gaze flew to Rick's weathered face. His blue eyes did not cast an accusing stare. Had he accepted Jack's version of the truth?

Rick laughed. "Paula and I teach a group of three-year-olds on Sunday mornings. I love those kids, but they sure have a lot of energy."

"Right," Jack agreed, his heart pounding hard against his chest. "I'm not a good instructor. . .for people. Training horses is more my style." He paused and turned his attention back to Kristi, still wishing he'd not been so terse. "Would you like to ride Rosie?"

Kristi tilted her head thoughtfully. "I'd love to, except I haven't been on a horse in about ten years." She grimaced. "Even then, I didn't learn properly. I'm afraid you might lose patience with me."

Jack felt torn between his decision to avoid friendships and a deep desire to demonstrate the well-trained mare. "I bet with your dad here, you could behave," he said with a smile.

She glanced at her dad then back to Jack before stepping closer to the horse. Rosie nuzzled her hand. "All right," she said. "As long as it's not too much bother—and she's gentle."

While Carlos, the head trainer, prepared the horse, using an English saddle and a halter under the bridle, Jack pointed out the various arenas and their purpose. Rick and Kristi were the first ones to see the completed facility, and he realized the value of community support. At least that's what he told himself.

While Kristi expressed her appreciation for the lab containing various medicines, bandages, and supplies, her dad appeared fascinated with the large tack room. Neither of them had ever seen a covered wash rack for bathing horses or a walker permitting them to dry. Jack pointed out the process was necessary for the hot Texas climate.

When Carlos led Rosie out into a covered arena, Rick received a call on his cell phone. He moved outside the barn while talking, leaving Kristi and Jack alone.

"Thank you for all you've done this afternoon," she said. "I appreciate it since we got off to such a bad start."

"No problem," Jack replied, conscious of the effect her melodious voice had on his senses. "This is good practice for me anyway. Are you ready to ride?"

She nodded, and he assisted her up into the saddle. Kristi

trembled slightly, and he wondered if she feared the horse.

"Are you nervous?" he asked, adjusting the stirrups.

"Maybe a little," she admitted. "I neglected to say the last time I rode, the horse threw me."

He raised an eyebrow. "Let me guess. You didn't get back on?"

Kristi wiggled her nose. "Right. Sure hope this cures me."

He chuckled. "It will when you decide you're the one in control."

Along with the familiar smells of barns, horses, and tack, he detected the scent of her perfume—a pleasant blend of woodsy and flowery aromas. He disliked what her nearness did to him. Masking his uneasiness, he took on the role of an instructor. "The first thing you need to remember. . ."

"I hate to cut this short," Rick interrupted a short while later, "but there's a problem at one of the building sites, and I need to take care of it." He peered up into Kristi's face. "I'm sorry, and you were about to make your big riding debut."

A brief look of disillusion swept over her face, but she quickly masked it with a grin. "I'll wait until you buy an Arabian," she said and started to swing her leg over Rosie.

"Wait just a minute," Rick urged. "Jack, I won't be very long. Do you suppose she could ride a little, and I could pick her up on the way back?"

four

Kristi felt a slow ascent of color from her neck to her cheeks. She knew her dad meant well, but imposing upon Jack equated her to the spoiled kids he had mentioned earlier. Suddenly the image of a twelve year old pitching a temper tantrum flashed across her mind. How embarrassing, and she was a grown woman!

"Please, Dad, I'm perfectly okay leaving now. After all, we've taken a lot of Jack's time this afternoon."

"I don't mind at all," Jack said slowly, but Kristi doubted his sincerity. "We can work in the training pen and possibly progress to a larger arena."

Her dad nodded and glanced at Kristi. Humiliation still reigned over her emotions. Once again, she looked like a fool in Jack's presence. She didn't blame her dad; he simply wanted her to experience the same enthusiasm for horses he shared. "It's really not necessary," she began, moistening her lips. "And I don't want to be an imposition."

"You aren't," Jack assured her, his gray gaze fixed on her dad. "The horse is equipped for a lesson, so let's not make Rosie feel she got all dressed for nothing."

Kristi smiled; perhaps her fears were unwarranted. If they could talk comfortably, then a friendship might develop. But she refused to ask him about photographing his horses.

After her dad left, Jack attached Rosie's halter to a lunge line in a round training pen. He instructed Kristi to perform a few simple exercises, and within a short while the mare trotted around the pen.

"How am I doing?" she asked with a laugh. Jack wore a

frown, and she felt at fault. "I feel like a kid on a carousel."

A faint smile tweaked at his lips. "Oh, you're doing fine. We may progress to the covered arena—for the more advanced learner."

So, you can be congenial without Dad, she thought. "I think it's the horse and the trainer, not the rider."

"Aw, that's what you're supposed to think."

And you have a sense of humor, too, she surmised. "Honestly, Jack, I'm impressed." She paused. "No. . .I'm more in awe of how you handle Rosie. To me, it looks like you raise an eyebrow, and she knows exactly what to do."

She delighted in the sound of his hearty laugh. "There's a little more to it," he replied, lifting his chin.

"Like the way you hold the whip and the tone of your voice?"

"Yes, and the words I use."

Kristi circled the pen again, wondering how many questions she could throw his way without closing the door to communication. "How did you learn all this?"

He seemed to mull her words around in his mind before answering. "When I was about ten, I started hanging around a horse farm near my home." He shrugged. "I imagine most boys fall in love with them at one time or another, but mine never faded. While the other guys sank their time into sports and girls, I studied horses. The caretakers took a liking to me and allowed me to watch them work. As I grew older, the owner hired me on as a stable hand. When I proved myself, they taught me how to properly train them." Jack observed her briefly. "Watch how you hold your hands."

Kristi adjusted her position, and he continued. "At one time, I wanted to be a jockey. All my hopes and dreams circled around riding a winning racehorse."

"And did you?"

A wide grin spread across his face. "Naw, I got too big."

Her eyes widened.

"A jockey weighs less than one hundred fifteen pounds. I couldn't seem to get my weight below one hundred twenty."

Her face saddened with the thought of his disappointment. "I'm sorry."

He continued. "Oh, but then I became interested in Arabians. I wanted to devote my entire life to these purebreds, but my big brother had different ideas. He wanted me in college, and since he footed the bill, I obliged him with a business degree."

"A success story," she commented. "Your brother must be very proud of your accomplishments."

"Not really," he muttered.

When he failed to say more, Kristi frantically searched for a different topic. Undoubtedly, she'd touched on a sensitive subject. "Okay, teacher, how can I progress to the next arena in my allotted time?"

"By being attentive and complimenting your instructor on his excellent technique," he said, with a hint of teasing.

Kristi feigned surprise. "Isn't that what I'm doing?"

A few moments later while holding on to Rosie's halter, Jack led the mare into a covered, rectangular area. Here, they had more room for the horse to trot and run.

Kristi knew time had escaped her. Her dad hadn't returned, and she didn't have her cell phone for him to call. "Jack, it's really getting late, and Dad should have been back by now. Can I use your phone to call him?"

"Sure. He's probably left a message on my answering machine in the office."

She dismounted with his help and handed him the reins. The closeness caused a shiver to race to her fingertips, and it shocked her. She didn't have any use for unbridled emotions, not in her carefully organized life. As they walked toward the barn, she noticed how the late afternoon sun picked up blond highlights in his straw-colored hair. She inwardly questioned his age. His slight build and boyish features made him appear young, but the tiny lines around his eyes indicated a man in his early thirties. She shook her head. His age didn't matter. In fact, she felt slightly annoyed and embarrassed by her attraction to him.

As suspected, her dad had left a message. The problem at the building site required major decisions and consulting with the client. After apologizing to Jack, he asked Kristi to phone her mother for a ride home.

Kristi winced. "Do you mind if I call Mom?"

"Yes," Jack stated firmly.

Her gaze flew to his face, but he smiled. "I can take you." When she protested, he continued. "No point in arguing with a New Yorker. I think it's illegal."

Kristi sighed, feeling humiliation needle her. Jack must think all Texans imposed upon their neighbors. "What about Rosie?"

"Carlos or one of the other trainers will take care of her. Any more objections?" His friendliness settled over her, and he did have an incredible smile.

"Suppose not," she said. "But I owe you two big favors for today." Neither the riding lesson nor the trip home included photographing his horses, and she dared not mention the latter.

"Wonderful," he replied. "I might let you clean out horse stalls at your earliest convenience."

Kristi wrinkled her nose. "All right. I can't be choosy. After all, you could have asked me to go scoopin-doopin' in your pasture." The idea of shoveling horse patties from his fields had no appeal.

Jack picked up his keys and chuckled. "I like a girl with foresight."

"Have some more chicken-fried steak," Paula urged. "I don't want you to go home hungry."

Jack patted his stomach and grinned at the tall, auburn-haired woman. "I'm about to burst. Mrs. Davenport, you are one great cook. How do you ever manage, I mean the bed and breakfast and cooking like this?"

Mrs. Davenport set the meat platter back down on the table. "First of all, please call me Paula. And in answer to your question, I have a wonderful lady, Irene, who comes in and helps with all the baking and housework. I couldn't operate the business without her or my wonderful husband and daughter." She smiled at her family, then back to Jack. "I hope you've saved room for dessert."

He shook his head. "Don't know where I'd put any more food, but go ahead and torture me. What is it?"

"Caramel apple pie with a scoop of homemade vanilla ice-cream."

He groaned and glanced at Rick. "How do you stay so trim? I'd weigh three hundred pounds in a month's time."

"We both walk everyday," Rick said. "And believe it or not, I do watch what I eat. A few years ago, I had a heart attack, and ever since, I've been really conscious of healthy living. Once in a while, like tonight, Paula allows me to have a taste of days gone by." He patted his wife's hand. "But tomorrow it's back to carrot juice and salad for me."

"Believe I'd better join you," Jack said. He turned to Paula and added, "This has been a meal above all meals, and I thank you for your hospitality."

Paula's hazel gaze expressed her gratitude. "You are more than welcome. If you don't have room for pie, then I'll simply send a big piece home with you."

Jack hadn't realized how much he missed spending time with good friends. When Paula suggested he stay for dinner, everything in him revolted. Already, he'd stepped beyond the boundaries of self-preservation. But deep inside, he craved a sense of belonging. His decision to accept the dinner invitation reminded him of being a boy again and making the initial effort of establishing friendships at the horse farm. Back then he wanted it more than he feared his brother's disapproval. A lot of things about him hadn't changed.

To Jack's relief, Rick omitted the topic of church, other than saying a blessing at dinner. He must have finally realized Jack's disinterest in a so-called God.

The one matter bothering him the most lay with Rick's knowledge of what had happened at Kingston Hills. When Jack became serious about purchasing the property in Brenham, he felt compelled to level with Rick. Deceiving the man who offered better than a fair price for the potential Arabian horse farm didn't settle well.

Everything in Jack's world had crumbled and fallen—his reputation, his self-esteem, his relationship with his brother Rand, and his faith in God. Understanding nothing would ever be the same again, Jack decided to take on new ideals and resolves. He swallowed his fears and hoped he hadn't made a grave error in revealing his past to the one man who could destroy him in Brenham.

Taking a sideways glance at Kristi caused him to wonder if he'd lost his senses. A beautiful girl, full of life and vitality—and entirely too likeable. He saw something in her brown eyes once evident in himself. Trust. How sad she must someday face the truth about God.

Picking up his cup, he took a sip of coffee. What a slim line he must walk between not offending this family and protecting himself.

"Jack, would you like a tour of our little business?" Paula asked. "I'd love to show you our home, and Rick or Kristi could take you around outside."

"Keifer, our resident hayride driver, should be hitching up Floyd and Boyd for tonight's trek around the property," Rick added. "He's one character—sings to the guests during the entire ride."

Jack hesitated. A sick feeling flopped around in his stomach.

He'd already gone too far. With an inward sigh, he resigned himself to viewing Country Charm. "Sure," he replied, feigning enthusiasm.

Much later, when Jack crawled into bed, his mind swept back over the day. He had to admit, the bed and breakfast looked inviting and cheery. The sun porch seemed to be his favorite room with its hardwood floors, red-paneled walls, furniture pieces painted green and white, and the white denim sofa and chair. Throughout the house, antiques and quilts gave the house a warm feeling, and he'd been amazed with each one of the guest's bedrooms. Two of them were frilly, feminine rooms, but the Texas room with a gun and sword collection and another room decorated with Stephen F. Austin, Washington County, and Brenham memorabilia caught his eye. Just when he thought he'd seen it all, Harry curled up beside a yellow and orange cat named Tapestry for a short snooze.

Jack could justify involving himself in every activity and request with his new friends except his attraction to Kristi. He'd sealed her smile in memory and couldn't put aside the arresting way her brown eyes sparkled when she teased him. More disturbing, he hadn't been enticed by a woman in a long while, and now the timing was all wrong. He'd best put his emotions in check along with all of his other conclusions.

❦

Sunday afternoon, Kristi examined the rules for the photography contest. She had the equipment necessary to take the shots, but her dad had made a good observation. The Arabians would be great subjects, except she hadn't gotten up the courage to ask Jack about using his horses. Scanning the awarded prizes, she surmised the dude ranch vacation still sounded like a vacation for her parents, but she wanted to enter simply because it challenged her ability as a photographer. Farther along in the ad, additional winnings whet her appetite. She read the description of a twelve-hundred-dollar camera awarded to the top two finalists. Kristi could have easily purchased the equipment herself, but withdrawing the money from her savings robbed her competitive spirit.

The ramblings coursing through her mind should have stopped her cold. Kristi couldn't possibly ask Jack. She sensed a particular shyness in the man, which accounted for the stone wall erected around him. Every time she felt him about to warm up to her or her parents, he backed off. Maybe his defensive attitude came from living up North. She'd heard since those folks lived in a cold climate, it reflected in their personalities.

There I go judging Jack by someone else's standard, she scolded. *He might consider it an honor to have his horses photographed and possibly viewed in a popular horse magazine.* Kristi sighed. How stupid of her. The horses of Bedouin Stables assuredly held national acclaim, either due to their owners' distinction or the horses' merits.

The idea of entering the contest refused to abandon her. Reading the deadline, she smiled. Plenty of time remained for her to make a decision. Besides, in a strange way, Jack Frazier fascinated her. She'd had her share of men throwing compliments and rivaling for her attention. In fact, she'd decided not to date any man until God put the special one in her life. Then why did the owner of Bedouin Stables make her feel eighteen again?

five

By Monday morning, Kristi realized the need to avoid Jack Frazier. His company invited disaster for her emotions. Her uncomplicated, carefully scheduled life didn't have room for a man tugging at her heartstrings. Too many things about him were a mystery. In addition, his unpredictable moods drove her crazy. One minute he laughed and joked, and in the next he acted like she had bad breath or something. How could she be interested in a man who preferred horses to people?

The attraction must be in his indifference, she determined. *He couldn't care less about me, which is why I can't get him out of my head. Besides, I barely know him, and it's against my better judgment to pursue any type of relationship with him. I do have more sense than this.* Her self-analysis made sense, but it didn't satisfy her heart. She stubbornly refused to pray about the matter, feeling certain God had initiated her decision to stay away from him. Jack didn't have half of the qualities she believed important in a man. Furthermore, he rejected her dad's invitations to church. Kristi had made enough mistakes in her life without the Lord. She fully understood the consequences of yoking herself with a nonbeliever.

Still, Kristi couldn't push Jack from her mind—the quiet, slender man with the gray eyes and gentle laugh.

At breakfast, her mother, dad, and Kristi lingered over their coffee. The bed and breakfast closed on Sunday nights, and Irene took the time off until Tuesday morning, which provided one restful day per week. Although Mondays were soon filled with errands, the three always put aside their schedules to enjoy a few private moments alone.

Her stepdad chose Mondays for them to read aloud Scripture and pray for each other as they carried out the week's activities. Kristi couldn't believe she had ever misinterpreted his kindness toward her mother as anything other than a deep-rooted love. Kristi's past accusations shamed her. To think she once considered the man a gold-digger, out to steal her mother's inheritance. He possessed more patience and understanding than she dreamed possible, and Kristi felt proud to call him Dad. Only a "father" would have loved her unconditionally after all the horrible things she'd done to him and her mother. Now Kristi cherished the day he walked into her mother's life and took on Kristi as a mission project. She felt certain the poor man needed combat insurance when he decided to help the Lord bring her back to the fold.

He finished reading from Galatians, chapter six, verses nine and ten. "Let us not become weary in doing good, for at the proper time we will reap a harvest if we do not give up. Therefore, as we have opportunity, let us do good to all people, especially to those who belong to the family of believers." He paused to pray. "And Lord, let us not get so busy that we fail to jump on board with Your will. Thanks for allowing Jack to spend Saturday evening with us. Guide me in how to help him. In Jesus' name, Amen."

Setting aside his Bible, her dad gave his wife a quick kiss. "What about lunch today?"

Her mother's hazel eyes danced. "You buyin'?"

"Of course. I'll even escort you to that new antique store outside of town—and then we can grab some ice cream for dessert."

"Hmm, I accept," she instantly replied, then glanced at Kristi. "Hey, honey, what's wrong?"

Kristi glanced up in surprise, afraid her mother might have read her bewildered thoughts about Jack. "Nothing, Mom."

Her mother tilted her auburn head and eyed her curiously.

"You were preoccupied yesterday, too."

Great, now she's guessed my broodings about Jack. "Oh, it's probably the four days of seminars scheduled for this week."

"Really?"

Kristi released a heavy sigh. "Okay, Mom, so you tell me what's wrong with me."

"Jack Frazier," both parents declared in unison—and shared a laugh at Kristi's expense.

Kristi frowned. "Don't be ridiculous. Why, the man isn't even a Christian."

With a sympathetic look upon her face, her mother slowly shook her head. "Sometimes our hearts rule our heads."

Wetting her lips and attempting to form the right words to halt any more talk about Jack, Kristi stole a look at her dad. Silently, she asked for sympathy, except she didn't really understand the emotions tugging at her senses.

"Don't look at me, princess," he replied, shielding himself with his hands in front of him. "Your mother's come up with this one all by herself."

Kristi settled back into the ladder-back chair and cemented her fingers around a glass of orange juice. "Dad," she began, "you know more about Jack than you're letting on, don't you?"

His crystal blue eyes softened. "What makes you think I would know anything?"

"Your prayers about him plus the statement about respecting his privacy." She nibbled on her lip. "Can you tell me anything at all? I know he's not a Christian."

Her dad reached across the table and took her mother's hand. "Jack is a believer. Some time ago, he ran into a whole string of bad luck, and he's been blaming God for it ever since."

Kristi saw a compassionate look spread over her mother's face.

"And you know about it, too," Kristi said, studying her mother's countenance.

Silence waved its wand around the room.

Finally her mother replied. "Yes, it's a sad story, Kris. Rick gave his word he'd not reveal the situation to anyone. I don't know the whole story, either, but I do know Jack has suffered through a horrible injustice."

She offered a sad smile. "I do understand, Mom, more than what you might think. All I have to do is remember my past. I'll pray God heals his heart and leads him back home. Besides, if I can change my ways, anyone can."

"From what I've learned from various sources, Jack's problems are not his own doing. He could use a friend, like we talked about before," her dad added.

"I don't think he wants one, especially me," Kristi said, suddenly losing her appetite. "If you haven't noticed, we have a knack of getting on each other's nerves."

He chuckled and popped a large, juicy strawberry into his mouth. "For a brilliant, educated, young woman, you, my sweet baby-girl, have a lot to learn about men."

"Oh?" she lifted an eyebrow. "Why don't you enlighten me then?"

"Well, he can't keep his eyes off you for starters," her dad said with a wide grin. "And I bet if you ask him about the photography contest, he'd be real obliging."

Kristi released her hold on the orange juice glass and used her fork to push a bite of scrambled eggs around her plate. Maybe it wouldn't hurt to initiate a friendship, and if he could benefit from Christian company. . . "All right, one day this week I'll stop over and ask him about snapping some pics of his horses," she managed to say while ignoring the smirk on her dad's face. "But anything else will have to be an act of God."

❧

Jack placed the cell phone back down on his desk. It had rung incessantly today, an oddity for a Thursday. A friend from back East wanted information on what to look for in purchasing an

Arabian. After promising to mail a few brochures on the subject, Jack volunteered to look at the horse before the man decided to buy. In turn, the potential buyer wanted to board it in Texas.

The call came both as a relief and pleasure. When Jack had no choice but to move his operation from New York, the threat of losing clients worried him. He couldn't afford to sacrifice many horses without taking a huge bite from his income. Granted, some animals remained stabled at Kingston Hills under new management simply because their owners lived close by. Those owners who remained loyal to Jack didn't care where he lived; they knew his commitment to excellence. He prided himself in knowledge and quality, the one thing Rand Frazier couldn't take away from him.

Jack exited his office and walked to the other end of the barn where Carlos and two other trainers groomed horses. The men worked ten horses a day then bathed the animals, sometimes a grueling task in the Texas heat. Jack did his share, too, with a hand-selected group of horses. During foaling season, he'd halter break at least five, plus train his normal ten. Most likely, he'd need to acquire additional trainers then.

The trainers working for him were a good lot, and he appreciated Rick recommending them. Carlos, the most experienced of the three, happened to be a nephew of the Davenports' cook and housekeeper, Irene. Jack learned that Irene's husband, Lupe, worked as Rick's foreman. They all were a hardworking family.

If he wanted a friend, Rick certainly fit the bill. In a lot of ways, Rick reminded him of his old friend Tom Manning who now lived in Richmond, Virginia, and owned a reputable Arabian horse farm. He was a Christian—a family man always willing and ready to help. But Jack preferred his solitude. It proved safer than becoming involved.

Now Kristi Franklin stood as another matter. Yesterday, she

drove by and waved as he walked toward his mailbox. His heart pounded at the sight of her, and it still bothered him. He couldn't shake those special things about her—the way she smiled and seemed to listen to everything he said. No matter what his feelings, Kristi did not belong in his life, now or ever.

Jack stopped and listened. A car door shut, and as usual, the announcement of a caller alerted him to possible trouble. Heading back to the barn's entrance, he caught sight of a candy-apple sports car and the slender young woman strolling his way.

Kristi. Her lovely face forced a grin from him. What had happened to his decision about avoiding this woman? She looked impeccable, dressed from head to toe in professional attire that heralded taste and expense. Cocoa brown hair lay in waves about the shoulders of her pale yellow suit. His palms grew sweaty. She looked less formidable in jeans and a ponytail.

"Good afternoon," Kristi greeted. "How are you doing?"

"Good, just busy." *Why does her voice have to sound so soothing?* he thought irritably.

"Can I take five minutes of your time for a question?" she asked, and he considered what a kiss would taste like from those full, plum-colored lips.

Stop it right there, boy. Those kind of thoughts will get you into trouble. "Sure." There he went again, agreeing to things he knew better than to.

She sighed and tilted her head. He recognized flirting when he saw it, but the sparkle emitting from those dark eyes didn't offend him at all.

"I. . .well, you know photography is my hobby."

He refused to respond. Chances are he wouldn't like what she had in mind anyway.

"Anyway, Dad found this contest in a horse magazine for amateur photographers, like me, and I was wondering if I could take a few pictures of your horses to enter it."

When he didn't reply, she continued. "He thought I'd have a better chance of winning if I had better subjects."

The suggestion of publicity about Bedouin Stables didn't settle well. "I don't want my business mentioned in any magazine."

Her eyes widened. "Oh, it wouldn't. The entry form doesn't require any information other than the photographer. No mention of the horse's name, its owner, or where it's located."

"Seems to me a photograph is a photograph. The talent shouldn't have a thing to do with the horse," he grumbled. "I'm too busy to get involved in such nonsense."

She stiffened and raised her shoulders. "I see. Well, it never hurts to ask. Thanks for listening. Sorry to have taken your time." Kristi turned and walked back to her car. She turned and lifted her chin. "You have a wonderful day, Jack."

He watched, hating himself for his rude behavior and realizing he'd just ruined his chances of ever seeing her again. Kristi didn't deserve this kind of treatment. *Isn't that what you wanted?* he asked himself. *To chase her away?*

The rumbling of her car engine broke the stillness of the afternoon, breaking the heavy air settling around him. He heard a horse neigh from inside the barn. A pesky fly rested on his arm. A trickle of sweat channeled down the side of his face.

Suddenly he felt more lonely and miserable than he had while waiting for justice in a crowded courtroom. . .or sitting in a damp cell. He had rejected her just as Rand and the others had scorned him. Innocently, Kristi had asked a favor, and with the force of an angry bumblebee, he had unleashed his sting. The past wasn't her fault. Had he lost all sense of decency in his cocoon of self-pity?

"Carlos, I've got an errand to run," Jack called from his office door. "If I'm not back when you fellas are done, then I'll see you in the morning." He shuddered, realizing his trainers had heard every word of his conversation with Kristi.

A few moments later, Jack drove his white pickup into the

driveway of Country Charm—right beside Kristi's sports car. He could only envision her fury with him. The last time they'd clashed, she'd sped away, leaving a cloud of dust behind her. This time, she'd driven home beneath the legal speed limit. He knew, because he'd turned and watched her leave. He could only imagine her seething, simmering anger. The kind that characterized erupting volcanoes.

Chuckling at the image of Kristi spewing lava, Jack emerged from the truck. *Guess I haven't lost my sense of humor entirely,* he thought. Laughter used to bridge him across problems and trouble, but he'd lost his humor in prison.

Harry, Paula's collie, bounded over to see him, wagging his tail and begging for a friendly pat on the head. Accommodating the dog offered a moment's reprieve of whatever he encountered inside the bed and breakfast.

Jack swallowed hard and headed around the house to the back door. The scent of roses met his nostrils, and he recognized the soft refrain of the old hymn "Blessed Assurance" as it floated from the gazebo. The song brought back memories of when his life had centered around Jesus. A twinge of regret pulled at him, but he quickly banished the thought. Those days were gone, never to be recaptured.

Procrastinating over what he needed to do, Jack cast an appreciative gaze at an ivy-covered trellis hosting the entrance to a small flower garden outside the back door. A calico cat chased a yellow butterfly across his path while honeybees rested on the tiny purple flowers of a Mexican heather bush. The homey atmosphere invoked around Country Charm calmed his turbulent nerves. Apologizing to Kristi might not be so difficult.

Giving Harry one last pat, Jack placed one foot in front of the other with his sights on the door. Suddenly it flew open, and a braid rug launched through the air; struck his face and shoulders and knocked him back onto the brick sidewalk.

six

Kristi gasped. Jack Frazier lay sprawled out on the sidewalk. Granted, in her anger she'd hurled the rug a little harder than necessary, but she'd never dreamed he would be standing there. Instantly the animosity raging through her body dissipated at the thought of what she'd done.

Pushing open the screen door, she stumbled down the steps and kneeled at his side. "Jack, are you all right?" she asked.

He slung the rug from his chest and examined the tiny pebbles embedded in his forearms where he'd braced his fall on the brick sidewalk. Wiping his hands on his jeans, he glared at her. "Did you pitch that at me on purpose?"

"No!" she cried, shocked he could conceive such an idea. "I wouldn't purposely hurt anyone. How could you suggest such a thing? I'm not a child."

"Right," he scowled. "You're stronger than a kid."

Her anger again bubbled near the surface. *Of all the nerve,* she seethed, *and I was afraid he might be hurt.* Kristi rose to her feet, silently ordering Jack to rot where he lay before she offered her assistance. In the next moment, her heel caught in a brick, sending her sprawling into a cluster of marigolds—with her foot still jammed inside the shoe.

"Oh," she groaned. Tears filled her eyes as an invisible knife seared across her foot. With a yellow marigold stuck between her fingers, she reached to lift her foot from her shoe. Beneath cream-colored hose, her ankle had already started to swell. She peered at it closely and tried to wipe away a smudge of dirt. Apparently, the darker coloring wasn't dirt at all, but the beginnings of an unsightly bruise.

Jack attempted to examine her foot, but Kristi stopped him. "Don't touch me," she ordered. "Can't you see I twisted it?"

"I'm not going to hurt you. I only want to see if you broke a bone," he insisted.

A burst of pain brought more tears to her eyes. When would her foot stop throbbing? "What are you planning to do, shoot me?" she asked, trying to wiggle her toes. "I'm not one of your horses."

He grinned, but she didn't find it at all funny. "I'm sorry," he countered. His words sounded gentle despite her frustration over the situation. "Let me help you up."

"I can manage by myself, thank you very much," Kristi replied, wincing as she shifted her weight and struggled to stand. The anguish became unbearable, and she collapsed into the flowers.

"Are you ready for a hand now?" he asked, his forehead wrinkled in concern.

"I keep waiting for it to stop hurting." She swallowed hard to keep from sobbing.

"Maybe you did more damage than you thought."

The screen door squeaked open, and her mother stared down at them in amazement. "What happened?" She descended the steps and bent at Kristi's side.

"I think she might have broken her ankle or possibly her foot," Jack said, pulling the flower from between Kristi's fingers and tossing it into the soft mulch. "Her heel caught in the bricks and she fell."

Her mother closed her eyes in disbelief, then reached out to the rapidly swelling foot. "Please, Mom, don't touch it," Kristi begged through a ragged breath.

"Do you think it's fractured?" her mother asked.

Kristi nodded, grasping both hands around her right calf as though administering pressure might stop the pain.

"I guess you would know," her mother whispered, wrapping

a loose strand of Kristi's hair behind an ear. When Jack gave an inquisitive stare, she continued. "She broke both arms and her left leg in a car accident about a year and a half ago."

He released a labored breath. "Well, let's get her to the hospital."

"I hate hospitals," Kristi declared, feeling like everything in her life had sped out of control. "And this is my good leg." She choked back a sob. "Mom, I'll take myself into town. You have guests, Dad's in Austin, and Irene's gone for the day."

"Let me take you," Jack said. "You can't safely drive anywhere in your condition."

Kristi wondered if he used that same soft tone on his horses. "I'll drive with my left foot," she replied, feeling decisively sorry for herself and not caring one bit. "Besides, it's your fault I'm in this condition."

His gray gaze stormed with indignation. "And how did you come to such a ridiculous conclusion?"

"Why. . .why. . .you started it," she sputtered. "I came by to see you, like a good neighbor, and you exploded like. . .like some tyrant."

"Well, I came back to apologize, didn't I?" Jack insisted.

"I don't know. I never heard an apology."

"You never gave me a chance."

"Stop it, you two," her mother said, frustration rising in her tone. "If I didn't know better, I'd think I was listening to a couple of preschoolers." She gave Kristi her stern attention. "I can put a note on the door and take you to the hospital."

"Paula," Jack began. "If you can help me get her to my truck, I'll gladly drive her to wherever she needs to go."

Her mother deliberated his request for a few moments. She sighed and studied Kristi's swollen foot. "Will you call me the moment you know her condition?"

"Mom! I'm a grown woman."

Her mother ignored the protest and thanked Jack for his offer.

"I'll put together an ice pack and get her old crutches."

Kristi watched her mother disappear into the house, detesting the thought of being alone with Jack—and detesting more the thought of him transporting her to the hospital. She felt his gaze pierce her soul. "What are you staring at?" she demanded.

"Oh, just you," he said lightly. "Seriously, I am sorry for the way I acted, and you have every right to be angry. At least let me make it up to you by helping out here." When she failed to respond he continued. "I'll behave myself. In fact, I'll even take you to dinner after the doctor bandages you up."

"No thanks," she mumbled, avoiding his stare. "But I appreciate what you're doing. Hauling me to the hospital would put Mom in a real bind."

"That's quite all right."

She forced herself to look at him, and he offered a faint grin. For the first time, she saw a dimple on his left cheek. "You know, you have a nice smile when you're not scowling about something."

"Yeah, you do, too. Really, Kristi, you could have broken your neck." He picked up the scratched black patent shoes. "Are these the same ones you left at my place?"

She nodded. "I think they're jinxed when it comes to establishing a friendship with you."

"I believe the problem is me." Jack paused. "I do apologize about this whole mess. My people skills aren't the greatest, especially when I'm in a foul mood. . .which is most of the time."

Kristi appreciated his admission—and his confession. "Thanks. And I did see you in better spirits on Saturday. Do we dare attempt another go at friendship?"

He said nothing, but she saw the longing in his eyes, and for the moment she forgot the prickling sensations racing back and forth across her foot.

Sighing deeply, Jack ran his fingers through his straw-colored hair. "I think I'd like to try."

ð

Hours later, Jack helped Kristi hobble back to the truck. X-rays revealed she'd fractured her foot in two places. The doctor wrapped it snugly and recommended she contact the orthopedic specialist in Austin who had taken care of her after the car accident. Memories of the time required to mend broken bones and the all-consuming therapy left her feeling depressed and weepy.

While Kristi leaned against the side of his vehicle, Jack positioned her crutches into the seat of the extended cab. "Slip your hand around my neck, and I'll boost you up," he instructed.

"You can't carry me," she protested. "You don't weigh over one hundred thirty pounds, soaking wet."

"Thanks," he growled. "But it's one hundred thirty five, and I am a little stronger than you give me credit for being." With those words, he lifted her up easily onto the seat.

"Oh, my," she said, feeling somewhere between embarrassed and shocked. "Boy, did I made a mistake." Kristi hesitated. "I'm sorry, Jack. It's just the idea of wearing a cast again makes me crabby, and then there's my job. . .and investing in comfortable shoes."

He crossed his arms and chuckled. "Considering the size of those heels, that might be a blessing."

The image of what she must look like—dirty clothes, torn hose, and her right foot two sizes bigger than the left suddenly seemed amusing, and she laughed. "I really look like the pro executive," she said. Glancing into the rearview mirror, Kristi cringed. "Wonderful, I have mascara smudged beneath both eyes like a raccoon and makeup running down my cheeks. Still want to take me to dinner?"

Jack's gray eyes sparkled mischievously. "Definitely. I'm starved."

"Me, too," she admitted. "How about a drive-through burger somewhere? The sign 'no shoes, no service' may apply to me."

He nodded and grinned before closing her door. Once he started up the engine, he turned to her. "Do you want to pick up the pain medication first?"

"Probably so. My foot really hurts. But I warn you, the last time I took this stuff I got silly."

"Sounds like an improvement over 'ouch' and crocodile tears," Jack replied, his gaze tender. He did have a gentle touch, and he'd held her hand in the emergency room.

Perhaps Jack Frazier isn't so bad after all, she thought. He'd taken care of her quite nicely and even listened while she wailed about having another broken bone.

After eating burgers, fries, and large drinks, Jack drove out of Brenham to the bed and breakfast. All the way home, Kristi felt herself slipping off to sleep, no doubt the side effects of the pain medication. He urged her to go ahead and relax, but she felt uncomfortable conking out in his truck. What if she snored?

"Just talk to me," she urged. "We'll be home in a few minutes, anyway."

"And what would you like to hear?" he asked. He'd talked freely during the course of the hospital wait and then later while munching fries in the parking lot of the local burger joint.

"Oh," she said slowly, realizing her tongue had thickened along with the droopy eyelids. "What about your horses? Tell me about your all-time favorite."

He inhaled deeply, as though searching his mind for the best Arabian ever to grace his stables. "First, I'd like to ask you a favor."

She glanced over curiously. In the shadows of night, she couldn't read his face.

"Would you consider photographing Desert Wind? I need

some good shots to pass on for breeding purposes, and you could enter one in your photo contest."

"Are you feeling sorry for me?" she managed to ask over the effects of the medication.

"Probably."

Kristi leaned her head back against the headrest, too tired to think of something witty to say. "I don't care if you are," she admitted with a weak smile. "And yes, I want those pictures."

"Of course, I'd get a share in the winnings," he teased.

"First prize is a trip to a dude ranch in Montana. Second prize is a great camera," she said, finding it difficult to follow his New York accent, or maybe the medication simply dulled her senses.

"I'd like the—"

But Kristi never heard his reply as she drifted off to sleep.

&

The next day, her dad drove her to the orthopedic specialist in Austin. The doctor found it difficult to believe Kristi had broken her foot in two places. "You either have a crush on me or you're addicted to plaster," he accused.

Kristi grinned at the sixty-five-year-old doctor with his single lock of gray hair at the crown of his head. "You've stolen my heart."

She rescheduled her seminars for the following week and fit them around already booked slots for the next. Once the word got around that she had "done it again," according to her stepdad, friends called and stopped by for visits. She welcomed them all, determined not to let depression rule her emotions.

Oddly enough, Jack phoned every day. He didn't talk long, but he always had a joke or clever story. Kristi looked forward to those little chats although they were never long enough to suit her.

On Friday afternoon she invited him to dinner. Jack declined, but after they'd talked a little longer, he agreed to join her for dessert in the gazebo.

"This is great blueberry. . .whatever it is," he compli-mented, after a second helping.

"It's blueberry cobbler, and I made it myself," she said. With her broken foot elevated on a lawn chair, they couldn't swing much beyond a few feet.

He lifted a brow, and she realized he planned a clever remark, but instead he grew serious. "You amaze me, all the different things you do."

For a moment she contemplated his words. "I never thought about it. I am rather eclectic." She glanced at him and saw a smile. "And if I see something that interests me, then I usually jump in with both feet."

"Like photography?"

"Yeah, or baking. . .or decorating," Kristi said. "I think most women are versatile."

He shook his head. "I wouldn't know. Both of my parents died when I was eight, and I don't remember much about my mom."

"I'm sorry," she murmured. "Who raised you?"

Jack shrugged. "My brother mostly. He's fifteen years older, and he didn't really need the responsibility of a kid brother."

"Oh, but I'm sure he loved you."

He sighed. "Yeah, sure."

"Do you see much of him now?"

"No. We don't have a lot in common. He's married with kids of his own, and I'm, well, I'm married to my horses."

Kristi laid her hand on his arm. The despairing look in his eyes made her want to reach out and touch him.

"Oh, don't feel sorry for me," Jack warned, setting his empty dessert bowl on the gazebo ledge.

She removed her hand, and searched frantically for an appropriate remark. "Doesn't sound like this is a pleasant topic for you. Shall we talk about something else?"

He stood up from the swing. "It's not necessary. I need to get going anyway."

"Jack, please stay. I enjoy your company."

He deliberated for several long moments before resuming a stiff position beside her. "I thought about something earlier today." He stared off to the left in the direction of a grove of pecan trees. "If you don't have plans for the morning, I could come by, pick you up, and we could work on those pictures."

She brightened at his suggestion. "How wonderful. I'll be ready at dawn."

He turned to gaze into her eyes, and she wished she could read his thoughts. Kristi smiled, hoping to put him at ease. Instead he rose again from the swing.

"I'll be here about nine o'clock," he said. "Thanks for the blueberry dessert. . .and for spending time with me."

With those final words, Jack strode to his truck, leaving Kristi puzzled and staring after him. At times his peculiar behavior caused her to want to shake him. Other moments like these, she could only label him as a hurting man who desperately needed Jesus. The mention of his family changed him from congenial to distant. It seemed he couldn't get away fast enough.

So there must lie the problem. A family squabble, she surmised. How could families treat each other so shamefully? A twinge of guilt settled over her. She knew exactly how loved ones could hurt others.

No matter what the root of Jack's melancholia, he needed to reconcile with God before he could ever take a step toward happiness.

She sat in the gazebo long after the stars studded a cloudless, navy sky, listening to the dulcimer hymns coming from the speakers above her head. In the quietness of night with the hum of singing insects raising their voices, Kristi prayed for guidance and direction.

She didn't know why Jack's relationship with his family and God bothered her so, except she'd once been separated from her heavenly Father and her family. The circumstances hurt. It had made her hostile and suspicious. She didn't trust anyone and despised herself. In the final analysis of those dark days, she had attempted to take her own life. Kristi didn't want Jack to walk through the same valley, and all she could do was pray that God would use her to help him.

seven

In the darkness of his bedroom, Jack fought a well of depression. He pounded the pillow and turned onto his opposite side in hopes his weary body would succumb to sleep. A part of him wanted someone to help him crawl out of the miserable hole choking the life out of him. A blacker side of him didn't care.

His bed creaked. *This is new furniture. It's not supposed to make noise,* he inwardly grumbled, wanting to blame his lack of rest on anything or anyone other than the source. He'd rather lie to himself than face the truth.

Kristi. Rand. His thoughts flip-flopped back and forth. Did she know the truth? Had Rick, in the best interests of his daughter, revealed what happened at Kingston Hills? Jack couldn't blame him—after all, a good father looked after the best interests of his daughter. Her safety and well-being should come first.

Jack sighed. He knew Rick hadn't broken his confidence because Kristi hadn't alluded to any knowledge of the trial and sentencing. If her father harbored doubts, then he would have persuaded Kristi to seek companionship elsewhere. The way Jack looked at it, the former owner either refused to accept the newspaper accountings and believed in Jack's innocence, or his Christian ideals outweighed common sense. Of course, Kristi, with what little he knew about her, seemed to form her own opinions about everything. But how could Jack expect her or Rick to believe the truth when he saw the holes in his own testimony?

They couldn't establish enough evidence in the new trial to prove him guilty. He had memorized the newspaper's reporting.

Rolling onto his back, Jack clasped his hands behind his head and stared up at the ceiling fan. Newspaper lies and Cassidy's accusations. Both ruined his reputation as a man and a Christian. He no longer held any credibility for either. Oh, he felt grateful for the loyalty of his friends who had stuck by him through it all. But he sensed most of them were more interested in their horse's care than in one man victimized by a family squabble.

Rand, his only brother, forbade him to ever set foot on his property again. His brother's words after the acquittal still rang in his ears: "I don't care what any court of law says. You're guilty, and I won't rest until you're destroyed."

Did Rand ever stop to think separating him from the only family he'd ever known topped the list of punishments?

Scattered thoughts about the past and present played havoc with Jack's mind. They came full circle to Kristi again. Why was it that each time he decided to dissolve their friendship, he relinquished? Something about her always drew him closer, and she'd slowly begun to chip away at the wall surrounding his heart. Now, he questioned whether he should add mortar and rebuild it, or try to tear the barrier down.

He couldn't bring himself to demolish the barrier. Perhaps he never could. Although he'd been released from jail a year and a half ago, the scars were still open and bleeding. It was too soon for healing, too soon to forget.

It occurred to him that Kristi's car accident happened about the same time he'd walked out of jail and away from God. Strange.

The longer Jack contemplated the mess of his life, the worse he felt. The misery consuming him dragged him on a downward spiral until he no longer felt optimistic about life—he hadn't since the sentencing. Scary, ending it all sounded like an easy way out.

Jack shot out of bed. He paced back and forth across the

room while stark fear clutched him in a vise. Amid all the heartache during the trial and later behind bars, he had not considered self-destruction. The implication now sent shivers up his spine. Jack's fingertips tingled. He headed to the kitchen for a glass of water—ice water.

I'm not giving up on me yet, he determined. Pounding his fist on the countertop, he recalled his old beliefs about God. Back then, Jack thought obedience, trust, and faith protected every Christian against harm, but he'd been sadly mistaken.

Rand had deserted him, and Cassidy had lied to protect her own skin; but that didn't mean the end had come for Jack.

As far as the present, he planned to establish an even better Arabian horse farm than the one in New York. He knew the right people, and he knew what it took to raise purebred Arabians. His excellent standing may have been tarnished but not his dedication to the breed.

He wished his new friendship with Kristi didn't have to revolve around his past. A definite attraction to her had caused him to make a few bad decisions. Personal relationships spelled trouble. Somehow he'd make it through the photography session, then he'd steer clear of her and the Davenports except for neighborhood pleasantries. Staying away from Kristi looked like the only way he could rid her from his mind. When and if she ever learned the truth about him, she'd be repulsed just like the others.

❧

Kristi double-checked the things she needed for the morning: her new 35-mm camera, two rolls of twenty-four exposure color film, a tripod, and sunscreen. She handed the latter to Jack and pointed out the sunburn on his arms along with a quick lecture on skin cancer.

"And you're sure you have all the stuff you need to make Desert Wind look good?" Jack asked, peering over her shoulder. "From experience, I know photographers always need more film or another piece of equipment."

She took a deep breath. "I think I'm set." Closing her leather camera case, she hoisted it onto her left shoulder. "Remember, I'm really a novice at this. The magazine ad says only amateurs should enter the contest."

"I see," he replied, lifting the case from her shoulder and releasing a heavy sigh. "Ms. Amateur Photographer, you don't need to carry this thing, unless you intend to break the other foot."

"I'm used to taking care of myself."

"And a fine job you do of it, too," he said, offering her the crutches.

Laughing, they started for the back door through the country kitchen of the bed and breakfast. Both were dressed in khaki shorts and T-shirts. A navy blue, cloth "boot" fit over her broken foot and protected the cast but left a lot to be desired in the way of fashion. Jack paused and snapped his fingers. "Chocolate."

"Chocolate? For Desert Wind?"

His gray gaze swept across the red and green room, so homey and warm, right down to the rooster weather vane perched on the counter. He didn't want this warmth to end, not yet. "No, silly, for me. I never take on a project without plenty of solid, milk chocolate."

She winced. "Fresh out, but Irene baked a ton of chocolate chip cookies yesterday."

"Umm, perfect. Do they have nuts?"

"No." She wanted to laugh at the solemn look on his face.

"Good. I'm allergic to them. How many can I have?"

"As many as you can scheme away from my mother."

Her mother and dad walked into the kitchen from setting the dining-room table for breakfast guests. "I'll let you have a dozen," she announced, wagging her finger at him. "Only because you have been so helpful with Kristi."

Jack grinned and complimented her mother on her yellow sundress. Biting into a cookie, he shook hands with her dad.

"I won't have her out too late, sir," he teased as her mother placed several cookies into a plastic bag. "When's her curfew?"

Kristi loved it when he teased and joked. In so many ways, Jack Frazier reminded her of a little boy who never grew up. If only they could have one serious conversation without him getting defensive.

Minus two cookies later, Kristi and Jack piled into the truck and headed down the road to Bedouin Stables. Already the sun radiated a special kind of Texas heat, guaranteeing the day would be a scorcher.

Once at Jack's place, Kristi felt the exhilaration of snapping pictures and observing the magnificent horses. "Early morning or late afternoon sun is best," she explained while Jack helped her from his pickup and made sure she could maneuver on her crutches. "Plus, we'll perspire less now."

Already beads of sweat formed on Jack's brow and dripped onto his sunglasses. "I've never drunk so much water in my life," he moaned. "Will I ever get used to this heat?" He stared up into a cloudless sky.

"Most likely, but hot is hot, no matter where you're from." Already her neck felt warm, even with her ponytail pulled through the back of a University of Texas baseball cap.

He gathered up her equipment from the truck bed, and they made their way to the main barn. The smell of horses and tack met her nostrils, further heightening her enthusiasm for the project ahead. Music rang from a radio on the opposite end where Carlos put the finishing touches on grooming Desert Wind.

Jack frowned. "Some days I wonder if he's trying to convert the horses with his Christian music."

"I enjoy it. Calms me down or perks me up. I take it you don't care for the style?" she asked, baiting Jack for a statement about his faith.

"Not really," he replied, setting her tripod down outside his office door. "Makes me feel like I'm getting hit over the head with a Bible." He combed his fingers through his light hair. "I'm going to grab a bottle of cold water. Would you like one?"

She nodded and smiled. Jack seemed nervous, or maybe distracted best described him. In the short amount of time they had spent together, she suspected her presence bothered him. With an inward sigh, Kristi hoped he saw a reflection of Christ in her. She remembered her displays of temper. She hadn't done a great job as a shining example of Christianity— notably when a fit of anger took over.

He returned a moment later carrying their water. "Where do you want your equipment?" he asked, handing her a cool bottle.

She deliberated his question before taking a sip. "I think I'd like the barn in the background for some of the shots and open fields in others. You indicated you wanted some pictures. What kind of settings did you have in mind?"

"Doesn't matter," he said, after downing a long drink. "Desert Wind looks good anywhere."

She wrinkled her nose at him, and they moved toward Carlos and the stallion.

A short while later with the sun behind her, Kristi leaned on her crutches and positioned the camera on the tripod. She checked the F stop and moved it to F22 so the barn would be sharp in the picture. In other pictures, she changed it to blur out the background and allow the horse to be the focal point. If she'd given it enough thought, she could have started earlier when the dew still clung to the grass.

Jack stood at her beck and call, positioning the stallion and pointing out those qualities that made him an excellent example of an Arabian. Since she concentrated on taking the finest shots, most of his assessments were difficult to understand, but she mentally noted them to research later. Over the past week, Kristi had found several web sites providing interesting information about these horses. Jack had also provided brochures explaining some of the training techniques. Looking at other Arabian farm sites proved interesting, too, but she avoided searching on "Kingston Hills." She preferred Jack tell her about his former stables.

He stepped back when she signaled she was ready for another shot. Popping a cookie into his mouth, he continued his lesson on Arabians. "Note the size of the head," he directed. "It's larger in proportion to the rest of his body. And see how his wide eyes are located in the middle of his head? It gives him more brain capacity."

"I think he looks noble," she commented, snapping the picture and feeling the mid-morning sun warm her back. "I can almost see him leading a band of Bedouins across the desert for battle."

Jack laughed. "You must have been doing a little reading."

"Yep, this New Yawk friend gave me some pamphlets."

"Why you must be that purdy young thang from Texas," he drawled.

Yes, she genuinely enjoyed his company when they weren't fussing about something.

Two hours later, Kristi had taken all the photographs she needed. "Thank you. I don't know how I will ever repay you, but as soon as I get them developed, I'll bring them by."

He patted the horse fondly. "No problem. I enjoyed it. Do you know what would make a good shot?"

Glancing up, she shook her head.

"You, sitting on Desert Wind and dressed in traditional Egyptian costume."

Kristi laughed. "And how would you get me into the saddle or cover my cast?"

He frowned. "I'd think of something. With your dark coloring, it would be a great picture."

"I was timid on Rosie. Imagine how I'd feel on this stallion."

"Oh, I'm sure he'd behave. After all, he knows a beautiful woman when he sees one. You'd look like a princess."

She felt a tingling in the bottom of her stomach. What an unexpected compliment!

"Thanks, Jack. What a sweet thing to say," she replied. Men did notice her, but no one had ever likened her to Egyptian royalty. His words made her feel unique, and she liked it.

He must have sensed his words had an effect upon her, for he immediately turned and led the horse into the barn. From Kristi's point of view, Jack looked substantially uncomfortable. It bothered her—a lot—for now she feared his light-heartedness would sink to the moodiness she detested.

Oh, Lord, help me to say and do the right things, she prayed. Kristi slowly put her camera away and folded up the tripod. All the while she waited for Jack to return. No matter what his countenance, she resolved to maintain an optimistic attitude.

"There you are," she greeted a moment later. As she suspected, a frown had replaced his boyish smile.

When he said nothing, she talked on. "I'll have these pictures by Tuesday. Do you mind if I bring them by?"

"I won't be here," he replied, avoiding her gaze. "I'm flying to Virginia for ten days. Business." He stuck the tripod under his arm and carried the equipment toward the barn. She watched him march ahead and disappear around the building.

Kristi limped up beside him as he arranged her photography things in the truck. "Okay, I'll have them for you when you get back." She searched his face for a sign of the fun-loving Jack she'd seen before. "Hey, did I lose you back there?" She smiled, coaxing the same from him. A faint upturn of his lips greeted her. "You know, I'll miss you."

"Why," he asked, moving next to her so that they both leaned against the side of his truck, "when I can be such a jerk? Really, Kristi, I'm sure you have lots of friends around here who are better company."

eight

Kristi prayed for the right words. She saw the confusion in Jack's features—the way he clenched his jaw and the tic below his left eye. How could she get through to him? With Jack, she felt like she rode a roller coaster. He fought their friendship, then he took a step forward. Now he seemed disgusted with himself and recognized it was his own fault.

"I do have lots of friends," she stated firmly, studying his cloudy eyes. "I said I would miss you, and that is exactly what I meant." He started to speak, but she shook her head. "Please, let me finish. We've had a few misunderstandings, and I believe we share the blame for those. But Jack, we've had wonderful times in what little bit we've been together. I would like for those to continue." She tilted her head and nibbled on her lower lip. The urge to touch him became overwhelming. Slowly, deliberately, Kristi lifted her hand from its position on the crutch and rested it on his arm. "Let me miss you," she whispered. "I want to be your friend."

His gaze lowered to the dirt beneath their feet. His body heaved, and he raised his head. "I'm not what you think, and I'm surprised Rick hasn't already told you the truth. Being around me could result in some nasty publicity—perhaps damage your professional reputation as well as your Christian influence in this community." He paused. "I don't want you hurt because of me. I think too highly of you."

For some unexplainable reason, her eyes moistened, but she blinked back any semblance of tears. "I'm a grown woman— quite capable of handling bad news or gossip. All Dad has told me about your past is that you had problems in New York and you are a believer."

"Was," he instantly corrected.

Ignoring his response she went on. "My dad wouldn't reveal any information without your prior knowledge or permission. His word is his bond; he did ask me to pray for you."

Jack stared at her, his face devoid of emotion. "There's no need to pray. I don't have a relationship with God."

She smiled. "Sorry, I don't make any promises when it conflicts with my Lord. You may not think you have a relationship with Him, but He still waits for you to come home."

"Not for me," he said simply. "I take care of myself; it's more reliable."

Tears welled in her eyes. All the misery she'd endured while running from her heavenly Father scrolled through her mind. Oh, how she hated for this hurting man to experience the same agony. The lines across his forehead deepened.

"Jack, I want to help. Please, don't chase me away."

Silence, deafening silence. She couldn't speak without releasing liquid emotion, and she didn't want her tears to influence any response from him. Someday, she'd like to tell him about her time away from God, but not now. He might think she felt sorry for him, and possibly destroy any progress toward his healing. Jack needed to choose life before he could journey back to the Father.

"You are the most compassionate woman I have ever met," he finally said, brushing his fingers over her hand with feather-like softness. "I'm tempted to tell you all about me, but I need to think about this. Right now, I have to get you home. My plane leaves late this afternoon."

During the ride back to the bed and breakfast, she couldn't think of a single thing to say, and Jack offered no conversation. Even when they turned into the driveway of Country Charm, he said nothing.

Once they exited from the pickup, he pulled her equipment

from the cab and carried it to the back door. He walked slowly, and she wondered if his pace stemmed from courtesy due to her broken foot or if he wanted to talk. At the back door, he turned to her.

"I want you to ask your dad about my background," he said. The muscles in his face were drawn tight, and the tiny lines around his eyes intensified.

Kristi shook her head. "No, I won't. If there's something you want me to know, then you will have to tell me."

"It's for your own good," he said firmly.

She felt an inkling of frustration and swallowed the terse remark playing upon her lips. "I have had a little practice in judging truth at face value."

He glanced away, then back to her. "You have no idea what this is all about. Out here," he nodded at their surroundings, "you have a fairy-tale existence with no clue about the real world."

She thought of how little he knew about her, about how much her life had been immersed in the pleasure-seeking and power-minded goals of the world. "Maybe so, maybe not, but you won't even give me a chance."

Her words were no sooner spoken than he positioned the camera bag and tripod against the house and faced her squarely. "I want you as a friend, but I'm not sure I know how to be one." He turned and left without another word.

Kristi watched Jack enter his truck and disappear down the road. Part of her heart went with him. Would she see him again, or would he resort to becoming a recluse, content to hide away from anyone who might care?

❧

Later in the afternoon, Jack drove to Austin to catch a flight for Richmond, Virginia. Once he met Tom Manning at the Virginia airport, they planned to map out the next ten days. His old friend sounded so enthusiastic about an investor who wanted to import fifty Arabians from Egypt for breeding purposes. This man wanted Jack's and Tom's advice on selecting the horses and indicated a possible trip to Egypt for the three of them. In Egypt, the two friends could handpick the horses and help oversee the purchases. The opportunity cast a profitable outlook into the future for both Jack and Tom's horse farms.

Jack had thought of little else for the past several days, but he veered from telling Kristi about the trip. She'd already touched his heart, and he didn't want to invite more anguish by revealing his business dreams. He'd looked forward to the excursion until he spent the morning with her, or rather when he revealed his growing affections for her.

He still felt like a fool, and the thought of not seeing her again for ten days and possibly longer didn't set well. Things needed to be settled between them before he lost all sense of logic. His head told him Kristi should find some other man to occupy her time, someone deserving of what she had to offer. How much better it would be for her to forget him and his disagreeable moodiness, but his feelings said otherwise. He couldn't even break off their friendship today. And he'd tried. Truth is, he didn't want to stop seeing her.

A stronger man could have handled the circumstances much better. He should have made it clear she wasn't welcome in his life. But no, he made stupid comments revealing what he wanted to deny. It all sounded right at the time. She would look perfect posed as an Egyptian princess seated on Desert Wind.

Perhaps his mind had been too consumed with the business deal with Tom—acquiring purebred Arabians and a trip to the Middle East—for him to make sense of his personal life.

What happened to his resolve? He'd known her for little over a month, and she had successfully planted herself in his life. Despite the fact that they usually fought, the quarrels were his fault. Kristi tried to befriend him, and he drew her closer with one hand and then pushed her away with the other. How could any woman in her right mind put up with such nonsense?

The next ten days away from her should confirm his sensible conclusions. As long as people felt he belonged behind bars, he did not need a woman in his life—neither did a woman need him.

Unfortunately, Jack had jumped in over his head when it came to Kristi Franklin. How could one man, so focused on all the problems of his life, find himself completely charmed by one woman? He'd become a bigger idiot than he thought possible.

Once onboard the plane, a flight attendant in first class approached him. "Sir, would you like something to drink before take-off?" She smiled as instructed by the airlines, but it didn't look or feel real. Not like Kristi's broad smiles. Neither did the attendant's pale blue eyes sparkle like Kristi's dark ones.

"Yes, I'd like some black coffee."

The young woman turned to greet the man seated on the opposite side of the aisle with the same rehearsed words. Did Kristi offer the same pleasantries to her other male friends? A jab of jealousy twisted inside him. Why shouldn't she? They surely showed better manners than he.

Maybe he finally got his message across to Kristi. How many times had he hinted at and exposed his nasty temperament? He'd been rude to emphasize his point. He ought to feel satisfied and smug, but instead Jack despised himself and soon sank into the familiar depression that seemed to drain the life out of him.

Closing his eyes, Jack leaned his head back. A steady throb pounded at his temples. The headaches began at the trial and continued to plague him. During the ordeal, he'd prayed to have them taken away, but like so many times he had asked something of God, nothing happened. Jack attempted to concentrate on the business trip, but his thoughts continued to return to Kristi. He didn't know if he was tough enough to fight what she did to him.

At the Richmond airport, Tom met him at the gate. Jack couldn't miss him, a huge man in any context of the word. The two looked odd together and usually brought a chuckle— the tall, red-bearded man who exhibited a fondness for fine cuisine and the slight wanna-be jockey.

Jack's brother, Rand, and Tom were roommates in college and had been friends ever since. When Tom discovered Jack's desire to raise Arabians, he'd fronted the money for him to purchase Kingston Hills. The endeavor made both of them rich and respected for their honesty and willingness to educate others about the fine purebreds.

Jack found it strange that Tom still associated with him, yet his friend managed to maintain relationships with both brothers. Jack knew the commitment to the friendships stemmed from Tom's Christian values. On more than one occasion, Tom urged him not to give up on reconciling with his brother. With a sigh, he hoped Tom didn't bring up the faith issues. The last time they'd spoken had ended in a stalemate.

Tom waved, his bald head glistening under the fluorescent lighting. "Hallo," he shouted, wearing a grin spread from one side of his face to the other. He'd come alone, for not one of his five daughters stood beside him. Couldn't miss those girls; they all looked like their father.

Seeing Tom lifted Jack's spirit. From the moment they clasped hands, Jack's despair melted away. "You look good," he noted. "Where are the girls?"

His friend chuckled. "Left 'em at home. We need to talk about horses in peace and quiet. They'll be waiting when we get there."

The two shared a laugh and headed toward the baggage claim. He felt good to be in Tom's company; he always did.

Once they'd retrieved Jack's luggage and left the airport in Tom's truck, nightfall settled around them. Tom suggested a late dinner and good conversation, alluding to Jack's aversion to airplane food. After placing their orders at a popular steakhouse, Jack waited for Tom to bring up the topic of Arabians and the business venture.

"We can meet with the investor Monday morning," Tom announced, spreading a generous portion of butter over a thick slice of bread. "His name is Fleming Donaldson, from here in Virginia. I think he wants us to accompany him to Cairo the end of the week."

"I'm ready, brought my passport," Jack replied, feeling a surge of energy at the thought of bringing new stock into the States.

"Seems like old times at Kingston Hills, doesn't it?" Tom said, opening a packet of jelly. "It does my heart good to see you willing to take this on. A long time coming."

Jack nodded. "Some things are getting better."

"Making friends?" Tom popped a huge bite of bread into his mouth.

"Oh," Jack hedged, "the fella who sold me the farm is all right. Lives down the road. He referred me to a couple of excellent trainers."

Tom swallowed and reached for his ice water. "So you like Texas?"

"The slower pace seems to agree with me. It's going to take a while to get used to the accents—worse than yours."

Tom laughed and leaned back in his chair. Jack hoped he didn't ask any more personal questions. Pausing, he couldn't think of anything new to ask his old friend.

"Appreciate you letting me be a part of this deal," Jack finally said.

Tom folded the corner of his napkin and wiped up a water spot left from his glass. He dug out another piece of bread from beneath the checkered cloth that covered the bread-basket. "Rand's not doing well."

Jack didn't want to know the details or, for that matter, any information about his brother. He stared into his coffee cup, a sick feeling churning in the pit of his stomach.

"He and Lena are separated."

Lena and Rand had been married for twenty-three years, and they were the parents of two nearly grown daughters, Jack's nieces. Jack's gaze rose to Tom's earnest face. "I don't want to hear about them," he said quietly.

Tom slowly nodded. "I respect your feelings. You know I hate this between you two, and I refuse to take sides."

"Then don't."

He cleared his throat. "Except. . .Rand's wrong, and I've told him so."

Silence lingered until the waitress brought their meal. Tom shifted the conversation back to the Cairo trip and the prospects of both of their horse farms taking on more worldwide recognition. After several cups of coffee, they left the restaurant and drove to Tom's home west of Richmond where his wife and family awaited them.

nine

Tom's wife, Susan Manning, a tiny woman and quite out of place beside her mammoth husband, hugged Jack, stepped back and took a long look at him, and hugged him again. Each of the five daughters, ranging from ages eight through thirteen, had waited up to see their uncle Jack and flung themselves into his arms. The youngest one, Jackie, named after him, promptly produced a bag of milk chocolate pieces in his honor. He'd always been fond of this precious family and treasured their friendship. Now, he realized how much he loved and missed them.

No sooner had Jack been welcomed than the girls were scurried off to bed in light of early morning worship services.

"Will you be attending church with us in the morning?" Susan asked, once the girls had disappeared. Their youngest daughter had previously questioned him about the same matter.

He glanced up at the petite blonde from where he sat on a navy-blue leather sofa in the family's game room. It wouldn't hurt him to participate in their ritual. "Sure," he replied. "What time do I need to be ready, ten o'clock?"

She nodded, obviously pleased. "The girls will be thrilled. We have a new pastor, and he's such a good speaker."

Jack smiled. Susan knew his stand on Christianity since the trial, but she didn't give up. She seated herself beside him and wiped invisible dust from an old trunk that served as a coffee table.

A crash sounded from the upstairs, and Tom stood from his recliner. "Think I'd better check on the girls," he announced with a frown. "Be back in just a minute."

"Some things never change." Jack chuckled as the big man exited the room.

Susan sighed happily. "It's been a long time since you've been a part of our family, and we've all missed you."

"Thanks. I didn't know how much I craved the old times 'til I walked in here tonight." His gaze swept around the room: the family pictures, shades of deep green and navy in the decor, antiques with a few added pieces, and the distinct warmth of love.

Susan's eyes moistened. "We've been praying for you, and I must say you look good—even with a sunburn."

Jack examined his arms. "My skin hasn't gotten used to the Texas weather yet. A friend pesters me about sunscreen."

"Must be a lady," she replied. "Well, I see some of the spark from the Jack we all care about, and I'm thankful. Welcome back." With those words, she blinked back the tears. "Time and prayer have a way of healing the hurts," she whispered.

"Possibly," he replied, not wanting to disillusion her with his views on God.

She pulled back and patted his arm affectionately. "You're here, and what better answer could we have?"

He nodded and attempted to suppress a yawn.

"You need some rest," she noted. "And I have your room ready, the first one at the top of the stairs."

Tom towered in the doorway and announced he had everything under control. "I'm beat, too. What do you say we call it quits for tonight?"

Jack crawled into the same bed he used to sleep in when he visited the Mannings. It seemed as though nothing had changed, but only a moment's reflection revealed otherwise. The Jack Frazier who'd held Tom and Susan's daughters on his lap, munched popcorn while playing Candyland, and willingly attended church hadn't spent time in jail. Those were the days of innocence and truth.

٭

Jack couldn't remember feeling this tense in church—and it didn't stem from the absence of a suit and tie, either. Other men had shed their dress clothes for a more informal style during the summer weather, Tom included. He couldn't put his finger on the problem. The back of his neck tingled, and his chest felt as though someone had decided to do bench presses on it.

Rubbing his palms together, he noticed the clamminess. It reminded him of his first date. Maybe he'd gotten a bug or something from one of the girls. Glancing over at the family seated on the pew beside him, envy gripped him. At thirty-one, he could very well have a wife and children, if not for his sordid past. Pushing those dreams aside, his attention was drawn by the pastor's booming voice.

"Today's text comes from 1 Samuel, chapter eighteen, where the Bible teaches us about King Saul's intense jealousy of David. The people loved David, and his popularity filled the king with envy. Even Saul's son and daughter were partial to him. David did his best in service for the king, relying solely on God to lead him successfully into battle. As a result, Saul schemed to rid David from his life—to destroy him. He was forced to run for his life, and for many years David dodged Saul's vengeance."

Sounds like Rand and me, Jack thought regretfully. *My willingness to do my best is what got me into trouble. David spent years living in the wilderness, running from Saul. I'm living at the opposite end of the country doing the same. How ironic.*

"But David never lost his faith in God," the pastor continued. "His thoughts, his praises, his confusion, and doubts are all written down for us in the Psalms. David never gave up on God keeping His promise that one day he'd be king of Israel."

Well, I have given up on God, Jack assessed. *Maybe if David had sat in jail, he wouldn't have felt so optimistic.*

"So how are you doing in keeping up your end of the bargain with God?" the pastor asked, leaning over the pulpit. "When you put your faith in Jesus Christ and trusted in Him for eternal life, what did God require of you in return? Micah, chapter six, verse eight says: 'And what does the Lord require of you? To act justly and to love mercy and to walk humbly with your God.'

"David got down and depressed just like we do. He poured out his heart to God, then obediently went about his business."

Jack bit back the emotion causing his lips to quiver. He remembered crying out to God when the judge pronounced him guilty and sentenced him to jail. He never felt a flooding of peace or an assurance of God's provision, only a gut-wrenching fear and hatred for the deceit surrounding him. It took six months for the truth to surface while he rotted in a damp cell among the worst of characters. Now, just how was he supposed to rejoice and be happy in those circumstances?

Pushing the pastor's words from his mind, he focused his mind on the trip to Egypt, viewing horses, building his business. . .and avoiding his brother. Suddenly and without provocation, an image of Kristi drifted into his thoughts. If she were here, she'd be absorbed in every word from the pastor's mouth. Jack could almost see her smiling in agreement. Poor woman, duped like the rest of the Christians.

Jack shook his head. He was sure glad he had escaped the false sense of hope, but why didn't he feel any better?

The pastor's message nudged him the rest of the day. He managed a facade for Tom, Susan, and the girls, but restlessness yanked him inside out. He kept busy playing games, telling horse stories, eating better food than what he prepared at home, and looking forward to meeting with Fleming Donaldson. At last the day ended. Jack concluded the problem rested with his old friends. They must remind him too much of the past. Surely he wouldn't have to sever ties with them, too.

Monday's meeting went better than anticipated. Fleming proved to be personable and enthusiastic about his venture, but it irritated Jack to learn the tall, elderly man boasted of being a born-again believer. The idea of listening to someone spout religious platitudes all the way to Egypt grated on Jack's nerves.

As Tom had explained, Fleming wanted them to select the Arabians for him. In turn, he planned to divide his purchase between Tom's horse farm and Jack's, offering to pay handsomely for the boarding, grooming, and training of his horses.

"An opportunity of a lifetime," Tom said to Jack later that evening. "God is smiling on us."

Jack preferred to think of it as luck, but he kept his opinion to himself.

Wednesday evening at 5:57, Fleming, Tom, and Jack flew out of Richmond for a connecting flight at New York's JFK Airport en route to Cairo, Egypt. Fifteen hours later they arrived, weary yet excited.

A wild taxi driver wove them in and out of traffic, honking his horn every two minutes. Jack thought the timed reminders must have been a standard requirement to drive in Cairo. He started to offer the driver money to stop the car, but Tom and Fleming found the ride a source of amusement. The perilous trip finally landed them safely in front of an exclusive hotel.

During the next few days, they were ushered by private planes to various horse farms. Some of the Arabian owners wore typical Egyptian costume and others chose Western attire. No matter how they dressed, all were anxious to please and even more anxious to sell their purebreds. They paraded one horse after another for inspection, sparing no expense in entertaining the Americans.

Jack had never seen so many fine looking Arabians, and a desire for the same quality at Bedouin Stables rested in his thoughts. After each long day, the three men spent their evenings enjoying elaborate meals and making laborious decisions as to what horses to purchase.

On the fifth day, financial and shipping arrangements were completed, and in view of a crucial business meeting, Fleming took the next flight home.

Jack and Tom elected to spend an extra day to relax and stroll through the various shopping spots. Neither of them knew when they might be back, and this gave them a little extra time to view the city. At Tom's insistence, they enlisted a taxi to drive them to the open market area. Both men were appalled at the poorer section of the city and appreciated even more the living conditions back home.

"I need to find things for Susan and the girls," Tom moaned. "My name is mud if I go home without any gifts."

Jack laughed. "What do you have in mind? Did they give you a list?"

Tom fumed. "No, I don't have a list, and I hate picking out things without something to go by." He paused, obviously contemplating his dilemma. "I've got it. Earrings. I'll get a pair for all the girls and a nice bracelet or necklace for Susan."

Jack pointed to a modern store across the street. "Right over there is a jewelry store."

A grueling hour later, the two emerged from the shop with gifts for Tom's daughters. They were served tea and given personal attention unlike anything they'd seen in the States. Tom decided on the same pair of earrings for each of his daughters but could find nothing suitable for Susan.

"What about a papyrus picture?" Jack suggested, eyeing a store next door. "Or a glass bottle."

"Glass bottle?" Tom echoed, tugging on his red beard.

"Yeah, Egyptians are known for their glass blowing. She could put perfume in it."

Tom raised an eyebrow. From the look on his face, he was definitely not interested in an Egyptian bottle. Nearly another hour later, he purchased a papyrus picture of an ancient pharaoh for Susan. With a little more deliberation, he returned to the jewelry store for a gold bracelet. "Just in case she doesn't like the papyrus thing," he said.

Jack hesitated when Tom suggested his readiness for lunch. "I think I'd like to do a little shopping of my own," he mentioned casually. "Possibly one of those glass bottles you passed up."

Tom gave him a wry grin. "Shopping? Have you gotten yourself a lady friend?"

"Just a friend who's a lady," Jack corrected, avoiding eye contact with the man. "I won't be long."

"Not without me." Tom chuckled. "This has to be a first."

Giving him a threatening glare, Jack led the way into the lavish shop. He didn't know why he felt compelled to purchase a gift for Kristi. She might not even speak to him again. He'd toyed with the idea the first time he saw an Egyptian woman in native dress. He remembered his remark about Kristi dressed as a princess, and he thought it might be a nice gesture on his part to bring her back something of the area. A peace offering. He decided his first impulse to give her a native costume seemed too personal, but the nudging to buy something continued. He read an advertisement in the hotel room describing handblown glass bottles which an Egyptian legend said were used to hold the tears of those grieving the loss of pharaohs. Sounded like something Kristi might enjoy.

A short time later, he'd found the perfect bottle. It stood seven inches high, with swirled glass in red, blue, and gold. Unique in design with its hand-painted etching, the gift suited Kristi. Jack simply hoped she would accept it.

"Are you going to tell me about this lady?" Tom asked, as they walked back to the hotel.

Jack shrugged. The back of his neck grew warm. He despised the way he ran hot and cold with Kristi. Why couldn't he simply make up his mind to either pursue a friendship or leave her alone? Logic still insisted Kristi could do much better than him, but his heart craved the warmth of her dark eyes. He needed to make a decision now and stick with it.

"Well, Tom, at this point I don't even know if she's speaking to me. Every time I feel her getting close, I get scared and discourage any kind of a relationship."

"Because of the business between you and Rand?"

Jack nodded and stared ahead. "She doesn't know about it, and I can't bring myself to tell her."

"Jack, you were found innocent."

"I know, but this lady is good. . .you'd approve, which is another reason why I'm not sure how to proceed."

Tom sighed. "She must be a Christian?"

"Yes."

"God's trying to pull you back into His fold."

"I don't want God—or anything to do with religion."

"Christianity is about a relationship, not religion."

Jack sighed. "Yeah, I remember. It's simply not for me. So I guess I should discourage her permanently."

Their footsteps sounded along the sidewalk. Car horns blared. A man shouted in Egyptian alongside a café and waved for them to come inside.

"If you wanted to rid yourself of this lady, you wouldn't have purchased her a gift," Tom said. "Level with her about everything. In the meantime, my family and I will continue to pray for you, although you don't think you need it."

Jack cringed at Tom's insistence. "I'm as hard as those criminals I saw in jail," he warned.

His friend smiled. "No, you're not. A little misguided right now, but not hard." He paused. "I'm going to act as a big brother right now and remind you about something. If this lady is a Christian, like you say, she isn't going to settle for anything less than your rededication to the Lord."

Jack's mind grew numb. He only wanted friendship from Kristi, nothing more.

ten

Way into the night, while Tom snored, Jack reflected on his friend's words about Kristi. For certain, he needed to make a few decisions about her and abide by them. He'd never been known as a weak man before, but wavering in his decisions and actions made him sound fickle, and he detested the trait in himself. Sorting out his feelings and putting them in a logical format seemed like the best way to handle the matter. If Tom hadn't been asleep, he'd have flipped on the light to snatch a piece of paper and jot down all of his thoughts.

Number one: He did like Kristi. He appreciated her good looks, and although they'd shared in a few arguments, he appreciated her feisty personality. Her intelligence attracted him as did her witty humor.

Number two: If he elected to pursue a friendship with her, then he owed her an explanation of what had happened in New York. After all, delaying it couldn't stop the inevitable. Some day Kristi would find out if she hadn't already. After all, she did ask him to tell her the truth.

Number three: If, after a smooth ride through numbers one and two, Kristi still wanted him as a friend, he'd have to reveal why he felt negative about God. To Jack, it made sense that a mutual friendship shouldn't involve a difference in religious views.

Jack clasped his hands behind his neck. Seemed like he figured out things best at night with nothing else going on. Suddenly he wanted to talk to Kristi, hear her voice and honeyed laughter. Glancing at the clock, he mentally calculated the time in Brenham. *Hmm,* he thought, weighing the idea.

It's only six o'clock in the evening there. . .dinnertime.

He turned over to his side and studied the sleeping figure in the bed beside him. Throwing back the blanket, he reached for his clothes, wallet, and room key. There was nothing stopping him from making a phone call from the hotel lobby.

A short while later, Jack pulled a credit card from his wallet and began the process of punching in numbers to call the States. As he waited for her phone to ring, he wondered what he should say. Up to that point, he hadn't played with the words or put them together. Too late.

Rick answered on the third ring. "Country Charm," he said, and Jack could picture the silver-haired man smiling into the receiver.

"Hello, Rick. This is Jack Frazier. By any chance is Kristi available?" Why did his voice sound timid—like a wet-nosed kid?

"She's right here, Jack. You doing all right?"

"Sure, yeah, doing real good."

"Well, here's Kristi. Don't be a stranger now. Come on by."

"Thanks." Jack waited for her to answer. It seemed to take an awfully long time.

"Hello."

The melodious tone of her voice caused him to be even more nervous than before. "Hi, Kristi, this is Jack."

"Welcome back. When did you get home?"

He chuckled. "I'm still in Cairo."

"Egypt? I thought you went to Virginia."

"Well, I ended up flying here with an old friend and an investor. We're looking at buying horses."

"Sounds like fun. What time is it?"

"Let's see." He peered at his watch. "It's two-thirty in the morning. Did I catch you in the middle of dinner?"

She laughed lightly. "No, we just finished. Couldn't you sleep?"

"Not exactly." He hesitated and drummed his fingers on the

side of the phone. "I. . .I need to apologize for. . .being rude the last time we were together."

"Why, Jack, how sweet. Of course, I forgive you."

He felt himself redden. Yeah, he did resemble a kid. "Thanks. I've been wondering. . ." He paused. "When I get home in a few days, could we talk? I'd like to tell you about what happened a couple of years ago in New York."

"I'd like that very much. In fact, I'll look forward to it."

"Good. I. . .ah. . .appreciate you talking to me. I'll let you get back to your family now. Have a good evening."

"And you get some sleep," Kristi added. "Bye."

Jack hung up the phone and smiled to himself. Talking to her hadn't been so difficult after all. Maybe now he could put his racing thoughts to rest.

Once back in the hotel room, he silently went about the task of crawling back into bed without waking Tom. Feeling quite smug about his little trip downstairs, he pulled the blanket up around his chin and closed his eyes.

"Did you get to talk to her?" Tom asked, leaning up on his elbow. A hearty laugh rose from the large man's throat.

Caught. No point in replying.

❧

Kristi placed the portable phone on the kitchen counter. She'd been shocked a few times in her life, but not like this very moment. Never did she dream Jack would call, not after their last conversation, and especially not from a foreign country.

"When did Jack get home?" her dad asked, his crystal blue eyes sparkling. "I haven't seen your face light up like this for over a week now."

She wrinkled her nose at him and proceeded to gather up dirty dishes from the table. "He isn't back yet," she replied. "He called from Cairo."

"Oh?" her mother's interest sparked a chuckle from her dad. "Why ever did he phone from there?"

Kristi sighed. Now she'd earned the title as focal point of her parents' merriment for the evening. She might as well give them fuel. "He couldn't sleep."

"Told ya," her dad said and nodded to her mother. "Sleepless nights. A need to talk to a special lady. Our Kristi has him all topsy-turvy."

"Seriously," Kristi began, juggling a damp cleaning cloth in her hands. "Our prayers are working. He wants to explain about what happened in New York."

"Praise God," her mother murmured and glanced at her dad. "He's on the road back to God."

ᨠ

Jack drove his pickup out Highway 290 toward Brenham. It felt good to be home. Home. It had a nice ring to it. Tonight he could sleep in his own bed again, even if it did creak. And he mentally took note of contacting the furniture store in town where he'd purchased it.

To Jack's surprise, before he left Virginia, he'd invited Tom, Susan, and the girls for a visit. They'd agreed to come once Jack's share of the Arabians arrived from Egypt. He felt a swelling of pride with the thought of his friends seeing his horse farm. Smiling, he reconsidered his choice of words. About time he called it a horse ranch like Rick.

While gone, he'd been in close contact with Carlos, although he knew the man was quite capable of handling Bedouin Stables in his absence.

Picking up the cell phone, he debated phoning Kristi. The one thing stopping him stemmed from the fact that he'd committed himself to telling her the truth. Jack couldn't weasel out of it, and already he regretted his impulsive decision.

I'll call this afternoon when I get home, he told himself. *She's most likely gone in the middle of the day, probably giving a seminar.*

Mid-afternoon, after hearing about all the training progress of his horses, Jack seized the opportunity to compliment Carlos and the other two trainers on their excellent job during his absence.

"Rick Davenport told me you were reliable, but I'm the type who has to see for himself, and I'm really pleased. I know I won't ever have to worry about the stables as long as you are here to oversee everything."

Carlos grinned. Jack surmised the praise was long overdue, especially in light of his moody temperament. Leaving the trainers to finish their work, he stole away to his office to phone Kristi.

His heart hammered against his chest, and he wondered why in the world he felt compelled to put his weak body through such torture. For friendship's sake? *Sure glad I'm not in love with her,* he told himself. *I'd probably have a heart attack!*

Taking a quick glimpse at the clock, he decided to take a chance on Kristi being home by four o'clock. She answered on the fourth ring, just before the answering machine clicked in.

"Been running any races lately?" he asked, out of a lack of anything better to ask.

"No," she replied, with her typical little laugh. "My running shoes are on vacation."

"It's good to hear your voice," he said honestly. Taking a deep breath, he plunged into another question. "Do you have plans for the evening?"

"Hmm, I am busy for a couple of hours. I have a presentation to put together."

"What about dinner, say around seven?"

"Sounds great, nothing fancy though. Cinderella here still can't get her cast into a pretty shoe."

He enjoyed her lighthearted approach to her injuries. "I already made reservations at a five-star restaurant in Long Island. Can you call your fairy godmother to help?"

"No, sorry, she's on vacation, too."

He sighed. "Hometown cooking it is. I'll see you later."

Jack hung up the phone and realized his hands shook. *This is crazy,* he concluded. *I must have drunk too much coffee today.*

He picked up his stack of mail and began thumbing through it, discarding most of it in the trash. A knock at his office door easily took his attention from the bills and advertisements. He grunted a "come in" and waited to see whose footsteps came down the hall.

Carlos stood before him, hat in hand. "Gotta minute?"

Jack glanced up to see the frown on the man's face. "Sure, have a seat."

The head trainer sat stiffly across from Jack's desk. "I wanted you to know a man came here twice looking for you."

An internal alarm went off, but Jack refused to allow Carlos see his response. "Did he say what he wanted?"

Shaking his head, Carlos replied. "I know you don't care for strangers, so I asked a few questions."

"And what did you find out?"

"He's a newspaper man from Austin—following up on a lead. He wanted to take pictures of the horses and grounds, but I refused. Told him he needed to check with you first."

"Thanks, I couldn't have taken care of it better myself."

"He also wanted to know when you'd be back, so I told him you were traveling and had left me in charge."

Jack smiled. He did have a gem of a man in Carlos. "Perfect. If you see him again, let me know. You've done such a good job handling the situation, that I'll let you continue."

Carlos laughed, and Jack reached across the table to shake his hand. "As soon as things get rolling a little better, I intend to raise your pay to what I paid my head trainer in New York. Probably be by the first of September. I appreciate your loyalty; it means a lot to me."

Carlos left a moment later after assuring Jack of his willingness to help develop Bedouin Stables into one of the finest Arabian horse farms in the country.

Leaning back in his chair, Jack realized the media had discovered him—as he knew they would. He simply wanted to put off the public attention for as long as possible. It looked like only a matter of time before the papers splashed the story of the trial and prison sentence in front of everyone's eyes.

Good thing he'd chosen to tell Kristi the whole story.

eleven

Promptly at seven o'clock, Jack pulled into the driveway of Country Charm. Harry bounded up to meet him, eager as ever for a friendly pat. He obliged the dog and scratched him behind the ears. The diversion gave him a moment to settle his racing nerves. Reaching across the seat, he gathered up a bouquet of red roses—an entire dozen from Brenham's most popular florist. Jack headed across the manicured lawn and wondered if he should call for Kristi at the back door or the front. Due to his nasty display of ill temperament before he left for Egypt, he chose the front. She might still harbor a little resentment toward his moodiness. Not that he blamed her.

He grinned, recalling the time she'd tossed his keys on the driveway in front of his house and later on when she'd pitched a rug out the door, accidentally knocking him to the ground. She certainly didn't take any garbage from him.

Hope these flowers don't look like I'm interested in anything other than friendship, he thought. *After all, I do have the Egyptian glass bottle on the truck seat.*

Standing on the wraparound porch amid the white wicker furniture of the bed and breakfast, he rehearsed his words and how he should stand. Suddenly he wondered if his peace offering looked silly. No time for regrets; the door opened.

Kristi's eyes danced at the sight of him and the flowers. She wore a pale green sundress and one sandal. "Jack, you're quite the man about town—the front door and roses," she teased.

Words failed him. So much for memorized lines.

"Come on in. Mom and Dad will want to see you, and I should put the roses in water."

Somewhat embarrassed, he stepped inside the foyer and listened to the grandfather clock chime seven. What was wrong with him? He'd just returned from Cairo where he'd rubbed shoulders with some of the richest men in the world and now he felt like jelly—or rather jam.

Rick and Paula were busy in the kitchen entering data into a computer. Rick referred to it as the weekly accounting process, the means of calculating whether or not they were making any money. After Paula gushed over the roses and the initial greetings were made, Jack and Kristi made their escape and drove off toward Brenham.

"You look very nice," he commented from his side of the truck. "And you don't limp much."

She threw him an accusing glare, then grinned sweetly. "Thank you. I see your sunburn is peeling—all over the truck seat."

Jack glanced down at his arms. "Yeah, I resemble a fish, but I remembered to use sunscreen while in Egypt."

"Good. I'm glad to hear I have a positive effect on you. Can you tell me about the trip?"

"Well. . ." He proceeded to tell her all about Tom, his family, Fleming Donaldson, Egypt, and selecting the horses. "And I brought you back a little something. It's there in the box." He pointed to the gift in the seat between them.

Kristi gingerly opened it. She made such a fuss over the bottle that he felt himself reddening. "It's handblown, isn't it?" she asked. "And hand-painted?"

"Yes," he replied. "It reminded me of you. . .sophisticated, yet colorful."

Kristi laughed. "I'm taking those words as a compliment."

His heart pounded as fiercely as when he'd called her during the afternoon. "Oh, it is." Jack wet his lips. *All of this for a simple friendship?*

"Am I making you nervous tonight?" she asked, her mink-colored eyes large and innocent.

Great, I must look and sound stupid. "Maybe a little. I'm trying hard to be a friend and not act so defensive."

She reached across the seat and touched his shoulder, sending chills far beyond the air-conditioning blowing around the cab of his truck. "It's only me, Jack. Don't try so hard. If I decide to bite, I'll let you know." She paused. "Besides, I've had my rabies shot."

Jack laughed, but he knew it sounded shaky.

Kristi tilted her head, her long dark hair spilling over her shoulders. She'd worn it down, like he'd envisioned her those days in Cairo. "Is the problem what you have to tell me?"

His palms felt clammy. "Most likely."

"Do you want to talk before we eat?"

"I'm not sure."

"I think we should pull off the road," she suggested, turning to study him. "You won't be able to enjoy dinner until you get all of this off your mind."

Once Jack found a dirt road off the highway and had driven down about a mile to the other side of a stone, single lane bridge, he stopped the truck. Cypress trees shaded a trickling of water from the creek bed, inviting them to sit along its banks.

"Right there looks like a good place to talk," Kristi pointed out. "I think I can make it easily."

He agreed and stepped around to the passenger side. Assisting Kristi from the truck seemed simple enough, but the velvety smoothness of her hand sent his senses reeling. He felt extremely grateful when she did not comment on his trembling grasp.

Shortly afterward they seated themselves on a grassy area beside the creek. She said nothing, making him painfully aware of his mission to explain the nightmare in New York.

"Okay, here goes," he began. "I've been going over what I need to tell you for hours, but I just forgot it all." He chased an ant from his pant leg and took a deep breath. "What I have to tell you is. . .well a judgment call. It's the truth, but there are people who believe otherwise. My brother, Rand, included. What I'm asking you is to hear me out and decide for yourself if I'm guilty or not. And I understand if you choose not see me anymore after this."

She nodded, and he seized the tiny capsule of courage in the most remote portion of his heart.

"I told you before that Rand raised me after our parents died. Although he didn't always approve of my love for horses, he did encourage me to get a good education and pursue my goals. Right after graduating from college, I became a Christian. Again, he didn't share in my new faith, but he supported me. Rand married and had two daughters, Cassidy and Carla, both of whom I became very attached to. In short, those girls were like my own. I carried them around as babies and toddlers and told them about Jesus. Cassidy never expressed any interest, but Carla did.

"Cassidy shared in my liking for Arabians and often visited me at the farm. When she turned sixteen and started to bring some of her friends to ride, I began to sense some problems. I didn't approve of their cursing, smoking, and the like, but Cassidy assured me she didn't participate in their activities. I warned Rand about her new friends, but he trusted her to make appropriate choices. You see, Rand owns a computer business, and he's always been a workaholic type. Not much of a family man or one to admit his family might have a problem.

"One afternoon, Cassidy showed up at Kingston Hills with a couple of her undesirable friends. I made small talk with them, thinking they all could use a Christian influence. She asked me if I had any chocolate, something we both enjoyed. So I headed back to my office to pull out a couple of candy bars for her and the other kids. Halfway there, I remembered I'd eaten the last one earlier in the day and needed to buy more. I walked back into the stable to tell her, and that's when I witnessed her selling marijuana to one of the boys. I didn't know what to say. My emotions bordered between anger and shock. I ordered the other kids to leave and took her back to my office. Cassidy needed to see the path she'd chosen led to destruction. In the back of my mind, I thought she might finally see she needed Jesus.

"She lost her temper, and I told her I had no choice but to inform Rand. She became even angrier and left. A couple of hours later, the police arrived and arrested me for assaulting Cassidy. She'd contacted her dad, torn her clothes, and done a pretty good job convincing her dad and the police of my alleged actions. Of course, her new friends backed up her story." Jack picked up a stone and threw it across the narrow creek, feeling the force of anger race through him fresh and strong as though it had all happened yesterday.

"It was Cassidy's word against mine, and in a court of law she sounded like the victim of something vile and dirty. I went to prison for six months, until one of the stable hands came forward with information clearing me. Rand never did believe in my innocence. He vowed to make my life miserable in New York and did a decent job in ruining my business. I had no choice but to sell out and start all over again." Jack pulled a blade of grass and tore it in half. He couldn't bring himself to look into Kristi's face, to see the reproach in her eyes.

"Now I understand why you thought I worked for a newspaper," she began. "And why you didn't want me to photograph your horses. Jack, I'm so sorry."

He stared out over the water. "I thought I could put it all behind me, but my moods are horrible. I didn't used to be this disagreeable. . .as your dad says 'downright rude.'" Releasing a labored breath, he added, "I hate myself the entire time I'm tearing into somebody."

"Have you talked to God about it?"

He gazed into her face—peaceful, calm, no pretense. He remembered when he'd felt the same way, when love lit his path for all his responses to God. "He and I aren't talking, haven't been since I found myself in a cell."

She nibbled on her lip. "So you gave up on Him?"

"Yeah. He couldn't come through for me when I needed Him most." He stopped abruptly; enough had been said for her to choose.

"So, what do you think?" He attempted to sound light, but he knew better.

"I believe you," Kristi replied without a moment's hesitation.

He wanted to accept her words and the warmth they conveyed, except he feared she spoke out of blind trust, not logic.

"Is Rand a Christian?" she asked softly.

"No."

A bird called out, and a fat squirrel scampered up a tree with another right behind him. A faint gurgle rose from the water flowing before them, and he smelled a clean fragrance in the air. He glanced in the direction of a distant dog barking and viewed a warm sunset in orange and yellow. Its beauty captivated him, a diversion from the ugliness of his life, but the woman seated near him pulled him back to reality.

Kristi touched his hand resting in the grass. "God's right here, Jack, all around us and in our hearts. He never left you."

twelve

It had been a long time since he'd felt a stirring in his spirit—a tugging at his heart to cling to God. Jack stiffened. He could not; the old hurt and pain still clung to him. "I don't believe in anything but myself," he whispered, staring across the creek. "No point in discussing it."

The silence lingered. To him, it seemed deafening.

"We're friends, right?" she asked. When he nodded, she continued. "This life, that we're called to as followers of Christ, isn't about us—not our pain or sorrow or anything about us. It's all about Jesus, His glory, and His purpose. You may never find out why God allowed you to sit in jail for something you didn't do until you see Him face-to-face. And then again, He may choose to tell you today. What I'm saying is it doesn't matter. Jesus does."

Jack mulled over her words. "I used to believe those same things. In fact, I remember repeating them to other folks who doubted their faith."

"So you let Satan win?"

"Ouch."

"You wouldn't have taken what I said personally, if you didn't still believe." Kristi paused. "You've veered off the path, Jack, but only you can decide to get back on."

He offered a faint smile. She seemed so earnest. . .sincere.

Without giving him time to form a rebuttal, she asked, "Do you remember feeling this miserable when you were serving the Lord?"

He managed a ragged breath.

Kristi lifted her chin. "There's your answer."

"You don't mince words, do you?" he asked softly, hoping a little humor might ease the heaviness weighing on his heart.

"No," she laughed. "That's why you like me." Her countenance changed to seriousness. "I haven't always lived a life for the Lord, either."

He raised a questioning brow. "I just figured you ran down the aisle at the age of four and have been on fire for the Lord ever since."

She gazed into his face. The depths of her brown eyes revealed volumes of past pain. "After my father died, I blamed God for everything. I was one horrible prodigal. I hurt my mother, but more importantly, I grieved God. To hide my misery, I put all of my energy into power and money." She shook her head as though dispelling every agonizing moment. "Not long ago, I had a prestigious position with a stock brokerage firm in Austin and a lifestyle to support it. My income was triple what it is now, and I flaunted it like jewelry. You know the cliché about God having to break us before we come to Him?" Jack nodded. "Well, for me it took my stepdad, as well as breaking both arms and a leg in a car accident, to put me back on the right road."

"What did Rick do?" Jack asked, finding Kristi's story a bit unbelievable.

"He loved me, pure and simple. Dad showed me what unconditional love really meant. God hadn't gone anywhere; it was me who strayed."

"So, you think I'm running?"

"I can't answer that."

He picked up her hand. "I will think about this, and you're right about feeling miserable. Some days I ache all over. Thanks for not pitching me aside those times when I've taken my self-pity out on you."

"You're welcome," she said lightly. "And I am going to keep praying for you."

They said nothing more for several minutes. Jack felt ashamed of his feelings, his past behavior, and his thoughts about God, but he couldn't quite bring himself to talk about it. He still felt angry, and he couldn't bring himself to let go of it.

The sound of Kristi's growling stomach seized his attention. "I think I need to get you some dinner," he announced. "Or do we have a lion hiding in the grass?"

They shared a laugh, easing the tension between them. Jack helped her to her feet, and they walked the short distance back to the truck.

⁂

"Never have I eaten such a huge chicken fried steak, even at your house," Jack claimed, patting his stomach, "or so much mashed potatoes and gravy."

Kristi grinned. "Did you save room for pie?"

"Absolutely not," he replied. "I'm going to bust." He picked up a red-and-white checkered napkin that matched the tablecloth and wiped his mouth.

"But Jack, this restaurant is famous for its pies, especially chocolate chip."

He grimaced. "You're kidding." He glanced around to where she pointed and saw several pies in a glass case. A chubby fellow wearing a straw hat and sporting a toothpick between his teeth studied each one. Above his head a small blackboard read: "Pies sold individually or by the slice." Jack cringed. "I'm weakening."

"Thought so." She wrinkled her nose at him. "Let's take a piece back to my house."

Jack purposely gave her a shocked look. "A piece? Why lady, I'm buying a whole pie!"

On the ride back to Country Charm, they chatted freely. Jack hadn't felt this good in a long time. He really didn't want the evening to end. The truth known, he wanted more of the same.

"Are you keeping busy while your foot heals?" he asked,

not wanting to sound too eager for more of Kristi's company.

"Pretty much. I leave Sunday afternoon for a week in Houston. I have a four-day training session and a two-day workshop to give."

"How are you getting there?" he asked.

"I'm driving."

Instantly, he envisioned her plastered foot resting on the gas pedal en route to Houston. Then he considered her maneuvering all over the city. "I'd like to take you," he said.

She laughed. "You sound like Mom and Dad; really I'm quite capable."

He stole a look at her. In the dark shadows, he saw her stubborn chin. "I'm hurt. Here I am offering my taxi service to and from the big city, and you decline."

She glanced his way. "You're serious, aren't you?" When he responded affirmatively, she sighed. "All right. I'm a little nervous about it myself, but I didn't want to let Mom or Dad know. In their eyes, I'm still a child." Smiling broadly, she added, "The training session will be at the same hotel where I'm staying, and I suppose I could take a taxi to and from the workshop site. Hmm, one stipulation, though."

"Which is?"

"Go to church with me on Sunday morning," she replied.

"You drive a hard bargain, but I'm learning to expect no less from you." He swallowed hard. "You've got a deal. Just let me know when to pick you up."

Jack could do this thing. Church. He'd recently made it through a service with Tom and his family. It didn't hurt him one bit, but he did feel uncomfortable. Something about the atmosphere of worship created a sense of uneasiness. Remembering the pastor's sermon in Virginia about David's relationship with Saul and how the circumstance collated with his own life gnawed at Jack's spirit. Little chance another sermon would have the same effect.

❧

Kristi turned up the radio in the library and began to sing along with a collection of contemporary renditions of traditional hymns. She'd started to read but couldn't keep her mind on the novel. Ever since she and Jack had talked two nights ago, her mind had swum with thoughts of his past and of his need to walk with the Lord. She understood all too well how he felt, except she couldn't make the decision for him to align his life with God. He needed to do all those things, and the part of her who wanted to make everything right with the world must bow out. The popular saying that admonished "let go and let God" whirled in and out of her mind. It left her antsy, as hyperactive as a three year old.

"Sweetheart, you gone deaf?" her dad asked from the doorway.

"No." She grinned, staring into his tanned face. "I'm singing and wanted to drown out my own voice."

"I've heard you sing plenty of times, and you sound just fine. Say, you sure have been happy these last few days," he teased. "Glad to hear Jack is opening up to you. You're certainly accomplishing what I couldn't do."

Kristi reached over from her sitting position on a cherry Victorian lounging sofa and turned down the music. "I'm merely doing what I feel I'm supposed to. He's a good man, Dad, and I really want to see him right with the Lord."

He bent to kiss the top of her head. "I know you do, and I'm real glad he's taking you to Houston. Now, I will have less to worry about."

"I would have done perfectly fine by myself. Besides I made a commitment to the training session and to complete the workshop." She punctuated her sentiments with a nod of her head. "But I guess it will give us more time to talk."

"Especially after he attends church."

She sighed happily. "You know, in the beginning I took Jack on as a project for you—well, for me, too. I saw in him what I used to be. But lately. . ."

"Yes?"

She shrugged and watched the corners of his mouth turn up. "Oh, never mind," she said. "I'm acting like a teenager."

"And it all started with a photography contest," he commented wistfully.

Her eyes widened. "Oh, you want to see the five by sevens I'm going to enter?"

"Of course I do, and besides, it's a great redirection of our conversation."

Kristi ignored him. She and her mother had already discussed her attraction to Jack—something Kristi had never anticipated. Her past relationships with men had centered around their income bracket or the titles preceding their names. Superficial qualities. The one thing holding her back from Jack lay in his relationship with God. Kristi saw the spark in his gray eyes and the way he cautiously reached out to hold her hand. At times he became nervous and tongue-tied. At times, she did, too. Kristi already knew how God felt about the two of them. Jack must establish the Lord's priority in his life before they could be right for each other.

On Sunday morning, a mixture of excitement and anticipation tugged at Kristi's nerves as she readied herself for the worship service. She'd changed clothes twice, then scolded herself for thinking how she dressed would influence Jack's state of mind toward the message.

It may not happen today, she thought. *Can't push God. He has His own agenda.*

&

Staring at his frown in the mirror while he pushed his tie into a knot, Jack wondered if he'd lost his senses. He'd been up since four-thirty, roaming through the barns, and then finally saddled Desert Wind for a run just as the sun peeked over the horizon. It had been a long time since he'd watched a sunrise seated on a horse. The beauty of the pinks and purples fanning across the sky reminded him of the many times he'd ridden early in the morning to reflect on God's creation.

Odd, his thoughts turned more and more to the Lord lately. He knew his rock-hard heart neared softening. Some moments he fought it; other times he allowed it to happen. The process proved painful, and the assessment of himself and the pity embedded in his heart needled him. Right now he felt numb. . . and scared.

Due to guests departing from the Country Charm, Kristi's family attended the second morning worship service. Paula and Rick taught a Sunday school class of three year olds, and Kristi often helped. But not today. This morning she waited for Jack to pick her up.

He knew she'd look perfect, probably take his breath away. He didn't mind it; he simply wanted the sermon to be boring. Yes, so dull she'd have to poke him so he wouldn't nod off to sleep. Brimming with satisfaction at this image, he snatched up his keys and left the house.

The air-conditioning inside Brenham Community Church rattled Jack's bones. He shivered; no threat of anyone falling asleep in this building. Now he understood why Kristi wore a suit. After the musical portion of the service, the young pastor, named Greg Johnston, stepped to the pulpit.

"This morning I am using Psalm twenty-seven where David writes about his fears. Perhaps this ancient song rose from his situation with King Saul when the man hunted him down out of jealousy. Or it may have been written when David's son Absalom used treacherous means to try to take David's throne."

Oh, great, Jack thought, *another sermon about David. Do these preachers have no other topics?*

"The Lord is my light and my salvation—whom shall I fear?"

Humph, Jack mused, though he smiled all the while the

pastor read. *David and I share a few things in common, but trusting God worked for him, not me.*

"Do not turn me over to the desire of my foes, for false witnesses rise up against me, breathing out violence."

Jack felt noticeably uneasy, and he stuck his finger in the neck of his collar for air. When would the reading end?

"Wait for the Lord; be strong and take heart and wait for the Lord."

Pastor Johnston looked up and smiled. "While I read this passage, were you recalling the many times fear has gripped you, held you paralyzed? It may not have been fear for your life, but it could have been your livelihood, health, or something about your family. David knew those fears, and still God had him wait for answers."

The temperature in the church grew increasingly warmer, but when Jack glanced around, no one else seemed to notice. It suddenly occurred to him that he was the only person experiencing any discomfort. He remembered sitting in Tom's church and feeling God poke at his spirit, and he recalled the same push a few nights ago while talking to Kristi. He'd denied it both times—shoving the sensation aside in light of his own doubts. Now, Jack faced another choice of accepting the invitation to walk alongside God or to continue ignoring Him.

Panic seized him. What if God wanted him to serve more time in jail? The last he'd heard, Rand hadn't given up in his pursuit to see Jack behind bars. For some unexplainable reason, he couldn't separate serving God from rotting in a cell for something he hadn't done. Jack couldn't shake the feeling.

"Are you all right?" Kristi whispered. "Your face is flushed."

thirteen

"Oh, yeah, I'm fine," he managed.

She glanced at him strangely and touched his hand. It felt like ice. "Hope you're not getting sick," she whispered with a sympathetic look. "Should we leave?"

As much as Jack wanted to escape the convicting atmosphere of Brenham Community Church, he knew those sentiments were wrong. He'd simply have to endure it. Shaking his head and avoiding her prolonged stare, he turned his attention back to the pastor, but not to the sermon. Later, when he felt more in control of his senses, he'd contemplate his reactions to this.

Kristi moistened her lips and directed her attention to the service. She knew exactly what ailed Jack, and it certainly had nothing to do with the settings on the church's air-conditioning. Serious conviction wrapped its mission around Jack Frazier's heart.

Later at the bed and breakfast, they all enjoyed triple-decker turkey sandwiches and spinach salad topped with her mom's favorite homemade raspberry vinaigrette for lunch. Afterward, her dad helped Jack pack the extended cab of his pickup with Kristi's two suitcases, hanging bag, and two heavy cardboard boxes of materials needed for the workshop at the end of the week. Naturally her dad accused her of moving out.

As soon as the last box had been shoved into place, and her crutches were teetered precariously on top, Kristi and Jack headed toward Houston. She enjoyed spending the time with him, especially when he made her laugh. The thought of his relationship with God, or rather his lack of one, sprang across her mind many times, but she simply didn't feel comfortable bringing up the subject. No point hitting him over the head with the Bible. The morning in church had been evidence enough of that.

"So when do you get the shipment of horses from Egypt?" she asked, twisting her body in his direction.

"It will be a little while yet. There's paperwork to complete, and I've got to make room for them in the other barn."

"Excited?"

He flashed her a grin. "You bet. By the way, thanks for giving me one of the five-by-sevens of Desert Wind. You did a great job photographing him. Looks like a winning picture to me."

Kristi couldn't help but laugh. "Every time I think of the first prize, I ask myself, what would I do on a dude ranch in Montana? I'd have to give the vacation to Mom and Dad." She gazed into his boyish face. "You never told me what you preferred?"

"I'll decide later." His gray eyes danced. "Providing we win. What time of the year is the vacation?"

She tilted her head. "I don't know; I suppose summer. Winter would mean snow and bad roads."

"I'll let you know," he replied. "What about you?"

"I'm not greedy; I just want to win." She gazed out the window at the green countryside speeding by. Riding with Jack felt so comfortable. She turned and said, "I like you," without batting an eye.

He chuckled. "That's good, since I'm your chauffeur." He hesitated before taking her hand into his. "I like you, too."

As Jack's fingers wrapped around hers, she felt herself grow warm. Now why did she make such a stupid remark? She'd sounded like she'd just hit puberty.

"You're blushing," he accused.

Kristi wiggled her shoulders. "I don't think so. Besides, you need to keep your eyes on the road."

"Yes, you are. You're embarrassed because you said you liked me." He squeezed her hand. "Hmm, and here I'd planned to give you something special. Guess I'll keep my pet frog to myself, and it's my favorite, too. But I do have a lucky rabbit's foot I might part with while you're gone. Might keep those city fellers away."

"No need for charms; I always wear a garlic necklace when I'm out of town." *I don't think there's much of a problem with any city fellas,* she inwardly admitted. *But until you realize your need to restore your relationship with God, we have nothing.*

Jack assisted Kristi in checking into her hotel across from the Galleria Mall in Houston. Along with the many elegant amenities of the fine facility, the management pointed out she could walk to the various shops right from the hotel. The longer the list of the exquisite stores grew, the more Kristi wanted to venture their way.

"Do you want to help me hobble over to the mall after my things are delivered to the room?" she asked Jack. "Unless, of course, you need to get back."

"No. I have nothing pressing, and we can get dinner later, too."

"Well, I'm buying," she stated, as the bellhop loaded her luggage onto a wheeled carrier and disappeared. When she saw the disapproval on Jack's face she added. "You brought me here, and I'm buying dinner—no sass."

He shook his head. "You're a mess, but we'll see who gets their hands on the check first." He helped her adjust the crutches. "You're a regular Hop-Along Cassidy, aren't you?" As soon as the words left his lips, he frowned. "What a lousy play on words," he muttered.

Kristi felt her heart quicken. She promised herself that nothing would destroy their time together, not even a mention of the old Western movie star whose name was the same as Jack's niece. Using a lighthearted tone, she said, "Oh, but she's not going to spoil our afternoon. We've got places to go and things to see."

Jack took a deep breath. "You're right. I think we might even find a gourmet chocolate shop." He slipped his hand around her waist and whispered, "Thanks, Sunshine. Sometimes I need a reminder of my self-centeredness."

A sweet flood of thanksgiving washed over her. Progress. Staring into his gray eyes, warm and tender, Kristi saw more than a friendship. It thrilled her in one breath and frightened her in the next. She dared not encourage him, but wasn't that what she'd done by allowing him to drive her here?

Oh, Lord, what am I supposed to do now? Surely, Jack must know she wouldn't allow herself to become involved with a man who questioned his faith. Her gaze swept over his face. The beginnings of love were as evident in her heart as in Jack's eyes.

"Am I scaring you?" he asked. When she merely smiled in response, he reached for a stray lock of cocoa brown hair and tucked it behind her ear. The touch of his fingers upon her skin sent tingles to her toes. "I know the requirements," he murmured.

"I don't want you making any decisions because of me."

"I won't. I can't. But I respect the standards you set for yourself. This separation may do us both good; for without it, I might say some things prematurely."

She nodded and prayed while listening. Jack's journey back to God had to be for his reasons, not hers. He held so many hurts inside—things he needed to face and deal with on his own. Without the Lord, they would continue to fester and infect him in a prison worse than any jail he'd ever spent time in. . .one that didn't offer any appeals or paroles, simply a life sentence.

❧

Shortly after eight o'clock, Jack left Kristi at the hotel and drove back to Brenham. He felt a profound loneliness, leaving him empty, and it startled him. These feelings hadn't crept up on him, or had they? As a grown man well-versed in the world's priorities, he gripped reality with both hands. After all, logic ruled his life. These new emotions with Kristi tended to border on love, and love bordered too closely to God. Why did it all begin and end with Him?

He'd forsaken God, and now he'd fallen for a woman who centered her life around Him. She knew the consequences of having Jack without the same commitment, and she didn't expect or want him to turn back to his faith based on her reasons. A good Christian girl realized she'd have the Lord when the rest of the world deserted her. As for Jack—he'd be left without Kristi or the Lord. What a mess. He palmed his hand against the steering wheel. How could one woman get underneath his skin in so short a time?

Once Jack arrived home and crawled into bed, sleep evaded him. Memories of his life before Cassidy's accusation and his faith in the Lord flashed across his mind. He remembered all the times he'd approached Rand about Jesus, but his brother hadn't wanted to hear about a relationship with the Lord. Bits and pieces of Scripture rose and fell as the hours ticked by. It seemed his recollections all rolled into one jumbled mass of confusion.

All day Monday, more Scripture, passages from books, and different portions of sermon messages rolled across his mind like credits in a movie. He began to wonder if the film portrayed his life. The trainers' songs on the radio talked about running from Jesus, and the pieces of wood framing his barns and stables resembled crosses. When it started to rain—a slow, steady drizzle, he pondered over his life ebbing away without a purpose. More than once, he found himself leaning up against a stall and questioning why he'd ended up in this small community in Texas.

In the past, Jack believed God had a reason for everything. If true, then why did he spend those months in jail? Why had he been led to Brenham?

Rising before a faint glimmer of dawn on Tuesday morning, Jack took Desert Wind on a long ride. When the pale colors of yellow and orange crested the horizon, he stopped the stallion and stared out over the east. Magnificent. Did he honestly believe this old world didn't have a Creator? How foolish to consider otherwise.

Oh, Lord, our Lord, how majestic is Thy name in all the earth. Odd, Jack contemplated. He'd all but eliminated the Psalms from his heart and mind. Now he sang them.

He stared out over the picturesque scene, watching the beginnings of a new day, and reflecting on how he took so many things for granted. Patting Desert Wind's neck, he swallowed hard, wondering if he was strong enough to admit he'd been rebellious. . .and wrong.

The anguish of yesterday had happened for a reason. He didn't know why, but as Kristi had said, perhaps he'd never know. He hated losing Rand and the closeness they'd shared for so many years, and the thought tore him apart. He realized the Lord grieved because of the brothers' separation and because of his own stubbornness.

With a deep breath and a freshness of determination, he urged the horse across the pasture and on to the road—the one leading him to Country Charm and Rick Davenport. He needed a brother to pray with him.

As Jack rode into the driveway of the bed and breakfast, he suddenly wondered what he'd do with Desert Wind. Certainly Paula and Rick's guests would get a chuckle out of waking up to a horse in the front yard of their bed and breakfast. He spied a driveway post perfect to wrap the reins around. *Guess I'm a real Texas cowboy,* he thought, amused.

Swinging his leg over the saddle and on to the ground, Jack

noticed a weakening in his knees. He trembled. No need to question why. Like the prodigal, he'd decided to return home. The crumbs from the Master's table suited him much better than anything this world offered.

He walked across the yard wet with early morning dew to the back door. Already the faint sounds of a hymn floated about him from the gazebo. The Davenports were up and no doubt bustling about the kitchen in preparation for their guests' bountiful breakfast.

After a quick knock on the door, he waited. Although settled in his mission, his heart beat faster than usual. Jack heard boot steps across the hardwood floor of the sun porch. He heard the rattle of the twisting deadbolt and the door opening.

" 'Morning," he greeted a surprised Rick. "Am I in time for coffee?"

"Of course, come on in." He pushed open the screen door and reached out to shake Jack's hand. "What brings you out so early?"

"Business."

"Business? At six o'clock in the morning? Do you need a vet?"

Jack chuckled. "No, I don't need a vet." He saw Paula cracking eggs into a huge bowl. " 'Morning, Paula. Sorry to interrupt you, but can I borrow your husband for a few minutes?" He turned back to Rick. "If you don't mind taking a little walk, I'll explain."

"Go on, you two," Paula said, shooing them away. "Irene is on her way." She set the carton of eggs on the counter and reached for two huge, green mugs from the cupboard. "Wait a sec before you go; let me pour ya'll a fresh cup of coffee."

Shortly afterward they walked out across the yard, sipping coffee, and enjoying the slight breeze of the early morning.

"I'm wondering what kind of business would bring a man out on horseback before breakfast," Rick said, curiosity etching his words.

Jack yawned and shook his head to dispel any traces of sleeplessness. "God. . .and a deep burning desire to get right with Him."

Rick laughed heartily as they moved toward Desert Wind. "Has He been after you all night?"

"More like nearly two years."

"Well, how can I help you?"

Jack felt the seriousness in the older man's voice. "Pray with me. I'm afraid I've forgotten how. I tried this morning, but instead I cried like a baby."

Rick stopped and placed a hand on Jack's shoulder. "I'm sure you still remember. Sometimes our prayers are only feelings we can't put into words; it's the condition of our hearts." He pointed to a nearby bench. "Let's you and me sit a spell and talk to the Lord."

fourteen

Kristi had been up before six-thirty. Since breaking her foot, it took so long to bathe, wash her hair, and get ready to start the day. Of course, limping around on one foot was nothing compared to a foot-to-thigh cast and two broken arms. She remembered her mother brushing her teeth, helping her bathe, and dressing her. She'd certainly learned a great lesson in humility!

Adding a second coat of brown-black mascara, she stepped back to assess her makeup. Frowning, she picked up an eye brush and blended in the smoky colored eye shadow on her right eye to match the left.

"Better," she said. "At least now I don't look like I have a black eye."

She glanced at her watch, calculating plenty of time for coffee and toast before the session began at nine o'clock. The phone rang, and she hobbled over to grab it, seating herself on the bed and wondering when she'd ever be able to wear panty hose and decent shoes again.

" 'Morning, Sunshine. I know you're busy, but I wanted to give you a quick call."

Kristi smiled into the phone. She figured when Jack had asked for the hotel's number on Sunday, he might call, but she never expected him to phone this soon. "Hey. " 'Morning to you, and I am just about ready for the day." She heard the sound of clanging pans and voices in the background. "Are you at home?"

"No." He laughed. "I'm helping your parents with breakfast."

"You're what?"

110

"I'm frying bacon for this morning's guests."

Kristi couldn't believe her ears. "You must be hungry."

"Hmm, am now, wasn't earlier." He paused, and she tried to imagine him wearing a Country Charm apron and pushing bacon around on her mother's huge griddle. "I have something to tell you," he said soberly.

"Okay." *This must be important,* she surmised, and her heart quickened.

"Well. . .the prodigal has come home."

Kristi couldn't reply for the tears brimming her eyes and choking her words.

"Kristi?"

"I'm here," she sobbed. "Oh, Jack, I'm so happy for you. This is wonderful, absolutely wonderful." She reached for a tissue and blinked back the wetness.

"I didn't mean to make you cry, and I bet you've already put on your makeup."

She sniffed. "I did, but I don't care if it runs over my chin. This is the best news."

"Seriously. I couldn't hold out much longer. The Lord kept chasing until He caught me. And you know what? I feel so good."

"But I don't understand why you're at the Country Charm," she said, confused and yet decisively happy.

"Simple," he said, and she heard him crunch.

"Are you eating the guest's bacon?" she accused with a giggle.

"Taste test. I am here. . ." His voice grew quiet. "I am here because I needed a Christian brother to pray with me—to listen while I asked God for forgiveness."

She took a ragged breath to keep from crying again. "My dad is one special man. I don't think I could count all the people he's helped lead back to the Lord."

"And I'm standing here a changed man to vouch for one more." Silence wrapped around their conversation, and she knew without asking that Jack shed tears of his own. "Listen," he finally said, "you have tons of things to do. If it's all right, I'd like to call tonight, and we can talk more."

"Yes, please do." And Kristi meant every word of it. "You have the most beautiful day ever."

The day whisked by, and Kristi found it difficult to concentrate on the speakers and sessions. More than once she scolded herself with a tough reminder that she would be teaching the same material on Friday and Saturday. She kept thinking about Jack's journey back to the Lord and how his life would be blessed with his rededication.

I can hardly wait to talk to him tonight, she thought, *or see him on Saturday.* She wanted to believe his decision might open the door to healing with his brother, but of course Rand needed to want a reconciliation, too.

Repeatedly throughout the day, Kristi caught herself daydreaming about her and Jack. Up until then, she hadn't permitted those thoughts to ramble on without putting a stop to them.

Sighing happily, she tried to convince herself the elation stemmed from his announcement. But she secretly admitted her elated mood had a lot to do with them, together.

When did I begin thinking about him. . .in a romantic way? she mused, while leafing through the guest directory for room service. She decided to have dinner delivered in case Jack called. Some of the other conferees planned to take in a movie, but she hesitated to commit to any evening activities until she'd heard from him. It didn't fit her normal spontaneous course of doing things because being in new and different environments had always aroused her sense of adventure. Still, she reasoned, she had the rest of the week to explore and enjoy herself. Of course, staying in the hotel room allowed her to look back over the notes from today's lectures, absolutely necessary since she'd spent most of the day contemplating other matters.

Midway through a dinner of spinach enchiladas, Jack called, and immediately she lost interest in food. For the next hour they chatted about their day, covering everything from investment strategies to construction plans for the new horse barn.

"I told Carlos today about my decision for the Lord," he said. "I also apologized for my past behavior." Jack chuckled. "He said he'd been praying for me, and I thanked him. So to celebrate their boss's spiritual renewal, I took them to town for lunch."

"Let me guess, the chocolate chip pie restaurant?"

"You bet, and I brought home a whole pie for our afternoon snack."

Kristi listened while he reminisced about his life back in New York. He'd taken an active role in a host of activities ranging from business organizations associated with Kingston Hills to community affairs. He'd spent spare hours doing volunteer work at a children's home, tutoring the slow learners and teaching them all how to ride.

"Wow, you were one industrious man," Kristi stated, finding a new appreciation for him.

"Which made for juicy reading when the papers got hold of Cassidy's accusations," he added. "Those newspaper reporters went for the jugular."

"Have they bothered you here?" Kristi asked, feeling a steady stream of indignation for his defense.

"Not personally. They've been by my place, but Carlos is great at running them off. In my opinion, it's only a matter of time until they sniff me out." He didn't sound the least bit concerned.

"You're not worried?" she asked.

"Nope. I'll dodge them for as long as I can, but when it all comes out, I'll rely on God as my strength. I'm innocent, simple as that."

Kristi sprawled on the bed and stared up at the ceiling.

"You've come a long way, Jack."

"Well. . .I've got a long way to go. What bothers me the most is my family. I doubt if Cassidy's changed her ways unless she's been caught and forced to get help. And Rand's too busy to be a father."

"What about her mom?"

"Lena is a good woman, but she enjoys her social life more than mothering. The last I heard, she and Rand were separated." He sighed. "None of it sounds good."

"Have you considered contacting him, or is that like slitting your wrist?"

He chuckled. "Both wrists. . . Oh, well, enough of this gloom."

They talked on until he asked if she wanted a dinner date on Thursday. Kristi didn't have to think twice before accepting.

The next day, she again found it almost impossible to focus on investment portfolios. For the first time in her career, she labeled her job as boring.

During the next evening, Jack and Kristi discussed everything from childhood memories, favorite vacations, horses, Texas heat, Southwest cuisine, and his New Yawk accent. Later, she couldn't remember what they'd ordered. Jack held her hand and lavished her with attention. The dimple on his left cheek deepened, and his gray eyes glistened when he smiled. Being around him gave her a tingly, giddy feeling. She forgot about food as her mind lingered on her new friend who rapidly approached being her best friend. What in the world had happened to her?

ಣಿ

Three weeks went by, and Jack amazed himself by the way his former life patterns surfaced. The habit of rising and meeting the dawn in Bible study and prayer reappeared like second nature. And he felt wonderful. Problems with Bedouin Stables and the challenges involved in dealing with people still arose, but the issues resolved themselves. He found the joy and satisfaction he'd known before. Kristi helped fill the gaps in his life. He treasured their relationship and realized they had so much more in common than he could ever imagine. Whether they were engaged in long talks, sitting together reading in the Country Charm library room, or viewing old black-and-white movies, they treasured each other's company.

As soon as her foot healed, Kristi wanted to take riding lessons to cure her fear of horses. Jack could hardly contain his excitement, for then they could ride together.

❧

One Friday afternoon near the end of August, Kristi offered to cook dinner in exchange for the many times Jack had transported her to and from work sites. Earlier in the day, the orthopedic specialist in Austin had removed the cast, and she could finally drive. After purchasing groceries in Brenham, she arrived at Bedouin Stables just as Carlos and the other two trainers were leaving.

"He's in the back barn," Carlos told her as he headed to his truck and hollered good-bye.

Kristi placed the food inside the house. It seemed strange to be in the same home where her stepdad had lived for so many years. He'd sold the property to Jack completely furnished, so everything looked as it did before. She found it hard to picture Jack living there.

Closing the back door behind her, Kristi walked to the barn in search of him. "Jack, where are you?"

"Up here," he called.

Staring up into the hayloft, she squinted to see him through the brightness of the sun, which temporarily blinded her vision. There he stood with his hands on his hips, peering down at her. She laughed at his stance. "What are you doing?"

"Looking around. Do you want to join me?"

"No thanks." She pointed to her foot. "I intend to keep both feet out of casts."

"Congratulations. Are you still cooking for me tonight?"

"Yes, sir. I have a surprise for you, too, inside the house." She paused and gazed above his head. "Jack, I bet that loft is infested with wasp nests."

He glanced about him into the rafters. "Yeah, there are quite a few of the red variety. I'd better climb down before one of them takes offense to me invading his territory." He reached for a rope tied to an upper beam.

"My stepbrother Andy used to swing down with that," Kristi said. "Drove his wife nuts."

"Hmm." Jack yanked on it. "Seems sturdy enough." In the next breath, he grabbed it and shoved off, swinging across the span of the barn.

Kristi held her breath until he landed safely back on the loft.

"Sure you don't want to try this?" he asked.

She shook her head. "No, sir. I've broken enough bones for a while, remember?"

"Okay," he replied. "Don't know what you're missing though." He proceeded to climb down the ladder and ambled toward her, grinning like a boy.

Kristi couldn't help but laugh at his antics. "You know, Jack, there are times when you remind me of a desert sheik with the way you ride Desert Wind, and sometimes you remind me of a greenhorn cowboy, but today I believe you resemble Tarzan."

"Oh?" he asked, raising a brow. "Are you saying as a sheik I could ride across the sand and sweep you off your feet?"

"Sure."

"And if I was a cowboy, I could rescue you from the outlaws?"

"Sure."

"And if I was Tarzan, you'd swing with me and my monkey friends through the trees?"

"Sure."

He stood before her, his face inches from hers. Kristi felt her heart pound. The nearness of him drove her to distraction.

"What about plain Jack? What if he asked you for a kiss, would he get one?" He leaned closer.

"Sure," she whispered. "You might even get two."

Jack took both of his hands and cradled her face, gently pulling her closer to him. His lips lightly tasted hers, as though savoring the first sweet nibble of fruit. Kristi wrapped her arms around his neck. She'd waited so long for this moment, and she wanted it to last as long as possible. As his passion deepened and his hand slipped behind her back to draw her closer, so did his kiss, until they reluctantly pulled away.

Kristi stood facing him, trembling with the realization of what had happened between them.

"We probably need to talk," he whispered, taking a step back.

She nodded. "Over dinner?"

"Yeah." He ran his fingers through his hair nervously. "Warm day, isn't it?"

"Stifling. I think it's over a hundred."

He smiled. "More like two hundred."

fifteen

Jack and Kristi locked up his office in the barn along with the other areas containing valuable supplies and equipment. They strolled down to watch the horses grazing in the pasture and admire the western sun before walking back toward the house. Neither mentioned the kiss or the talk Jack suggested. At his back door, they stepped inside to welcome the cooler temperatures.

"You know, every time I walk inside, I think how blessed I am to have this custom home," Jack said. "When I bought it, my interest lay with the acreage and layout of the property, but Rick spared nothing in the design and quality. Most times I don't feel like I deserve it."

"It is beautiful. I know he lived here eight years before he and Mom married." She gave the interior an admiring glance. "Frankly, I like your light oak cabinetry in the kitchen better than the red ones at home, but it's simply a personal preference." She cringed. "Please don't tell Mom what I just said. I wouldn't hurt her feelings for the world. She has excellent taste and can take anything and turn it into something gorgeous. You should have seen the bed and breakfast when she bought it."

He laughed. "Your secret's safe with me." Jack looked around the kitchen. "So what's for dinner? And don't you have a surprise for me?"

She pointed to a large bag on the counter. "Right in there. And for dinner, I thought about grilled salmon with a dill sauce, steamed fresh vegetables, your favorite potato salad, and a loaf of fresh herb bread straight from Mom's kitchen.

How does the menu sound?"

"Fantastic," he replied, peering into the bag. "What is this?" He pulled out a three-pound, solid milk chocolate bar. His eyes widened. "This must be for dessert."

She crossed her arms. "If you eat all of that tonight, you'll be one sick fella."

"Okay, half," he conceded. He examined it again and stepped to her side to place a quick kiss on her lips. "Thank you, sunshine, and I seem to remember you asking for two kisses."

"Yes, I did," she whispered.

"Would you like another?" A smile teased at the corners of his mouth.

"Can't," she replied, taking a quick breath. His kisses made her legs feel like jelly. "You might label me as greedy."

He set the candy bar on the counter and took both of her hands into his. "I don't know if I can wait until dinner to say what's on my mind."

She teetered on her toes and glanced down at his fingers laced with hers. "I am one terribly impatient lady."

"Well, what do you say we grab something cold to drink and step outside for a moment?"

She nodded and he opened the refrigerator to grab two diet sodas. Kristi's mind raced all the while he poured the drinks over ice. Did their kisses mean as much to him as they did to her?

As he handed her a filled glass, the phone rang. Jack winked and answered.

"Yes. Hello, Tom. . . Great!" He took a swallow from his glass, and she washed her hands at the sink, contemplating what she could do in preparation for the evening's dinner.

"No, I'm not alone. Kristi's here."

She looked up and smiled. A warm feeling swept over her, and the knowledge of her love for him shocked her. Yes, she cared about Jack very much, but until this moment she did not realize the extent of her emotions.

"You'll have to meet her. Are the girls coming?" He grinned. "All right. I'll see you a week from tomorrow." Jack replaced the phone, and she dried her hands. "Tom and his family are flying in for a visit next weekend, bringing their girls, too." He leaned one elbow on the counter and observed her. "You will love this family, Kris. Tom cried when I told him about my 'coming home.'"

"If you think they're special, then I know I will," she replied.

He said nothing. "Are you still ready for our talk?"

"Absolutely."

They picked up their drinks and walked outside to the enclosed patio. Jack snapped on the ceiling fan and motioned for her to sit down beside him on a cushioned sofa. Kristi scooted in beside him, feeling like she walked on a cloud. Her own realization about her love for him seemed to echo around her.

Jack suddenly appeared shy. Twice he started to speak and stopped. "I feel like a kid," he admitted. He took a deep breath and placed his drink on a small glass and metal table in front of them. "Kristi, for a while now, I've felt and prayed about what the Lord wants for my life. I don't have all of the answers, and maybe I'm not supposed to have them yet. But I do know I care about you very much, and I wondered if you would consider praying about. . .us. . .a solid relationship."

Kristi couldn't stop smiling. Her toes curled and her heart attempted to take flight. She tried to form the proper words before speaking, but her mind went blank.

He continued. "I have never asked you about how you felt. So I apologize if this is premature."

She thought for a moment she might weep. "It's not at all too early. I. . .I would like that very much."

"Can we pray right now?"

She offered him her hands, and he grasped them firmly.

They had never prayed to the Lord together except for a meal blessing. She felt timid, a little insecure. Nothing at all resembling her normal, confident self.

"Heavenly Father," Jack began. "We come to You asking what You desire of our relationship. I know I care about Kristi, and I believe You have put those feelings in my heart, but I. . . we need to know for sure." He squeezed her hand. "I pledge to keep my actions and my feelings for her pure as You have instructed. Help us to honor You when we are together and when we are apart. In Jesus' precious holy name. Amen."

He brought her hands to his lips and brushed a kiss across her fingertips. "I want to be in God's will, and I'll wait for His word. In the meantime, I want to make the most of every moment with you."

Kristi seldom searched for words, but lately Jack had changed her normal reactions. She looked into his warm grey eyes and simply nodded her agreement.

ه

A week later, Jack ushered Tom and his family through Bedouin Stables, proudly displaying his new horses and property. Susan and the girls were accustomed to barns and equipment, but they were more impressed with Jack's huge Victorian home and swimming pool. One look at the aqua water and all of the Mannings were ready for a swim.

"Is it always this hot?" Susan asked, as they pulled their luggage from a rented van.

Jack chuckled. "Yeah, I've never sweat so much in my entire life."

"I bet you enjoy your pool," Tom said, wiping the perspiration from his full face.

"Well," Jack admitted, "I really haven't used it very much. Kristi couldn't get into the water with a cast on her foot, and it didn't really occur to me to swim alone."

"And when do we get to meet Miss Kristi?" Tom asked,

slamming the door on the van. "Curiosity is getting the best of me." He laughed. "I can't imagine any woman putting up with the likes of you."

Jack grabbed two suitcases from the girls. "Well, look at who's talking." And he nodded at Susan. "What did you do to get such a lovely wife, bribe her to marry you?"

The girls thought Uncle Jack's comments were funny which spurred on the teasing between the two men. While the Manning family dressed for swimming, Jack phoned Kristi to invite her to join them. She arrived as the family and Jack cooled off in the pool.

To Jack, Kristi looked lovely. . .perfect. She wore a long yellow sundress, sandals, and had pulled her long hair back at the crown, causing her mink brown eyes to appear large and expressive.

"Kristi, this is the Manning crew," Jack began, after he grabbed a towel and dried off. "The big guy is Tom, the pretty little blonde is his wife Susan." He motioned to the five red-headed girls splashing about in the water. "Hey, you bathing beauties, can you come here a minute so I can introduce you?" All five giggly girls exited the pool, dripping wet, and crowded around Jack and Kristi. "From tallest to shortest," he began, "Jennifer, Jill, Julie, Jasmine, and Jackie. Girls, this is Kristi."

The five Manning daughters oohed and awed over Kristi, just as Jack had suspected they would. They wanted her in the water with them, but she'd neglected to bring her swimming suit.

"We'll talk over dinner," she promised. "Go ahead and enjoy the water for now."

"Is Uncle Jack cooking?" one of the girls asked. "We never ate his food before."

Jack proceeded to splash her. "No, we're having home-style cooking in Brenham, and tomorrow night we're guests of Kristi's parents at their bed and breakfast."

"Oh?" Jackie asked. "What can we do at a bed and breakfast?"

Kristi laughed. "Eat some great food, jump aboard a hayride—and the driver will sing for you—check out a petting zoo, go fishing, and take a long walk back to a creek."

Jack grinned at her. The Mannings had found a friend for life.

❧

On Sunday morning, the guests attended Brenham Community Church. After a barbecue lunch at Bedouin Stables, compliments of Jack and Kristi, the men drew aside to talk business. The girls went swimming while Susan and Kristi chose to watch them from under a nearby canopied table.

"Kristi, this has been such a wonderful weekend. Thank you so much for helping Jack entertain us. Fortunately, with this pool, the girls are nicely occupied," Susan said, taking a sip of sun-brewed ice tea.

"You are most welcome," Kristi replied. She'd already decided the Mannings were great people, and she felt an instant friendship with Susan. "I think it's more fun for us."

They watched the girls for a moment. Jack had found a water volleyball net in the garage and had strung it across the pool for them.

"Jack's change is a real miracle. I don't remember him ever being so happy, even at Kingston Hills. Of course, it's all because he's walking with the Lord again, but he told Tom that you have played a crucial role in this." Susan's voice spoke quietly above the excited screams of her daughters.

Kristi hesitated to reply. She didn't know how much to say. "He's definitely worth every moment we've spent together. I've never met anyone like him."

Susan laughed lightly. "Well, he's unique and very special to us. In case you haven't figured it out, our youngest is named after her uncle Jack." She turned to face Kristi. "Seriously, are you two. . .oh. . .hmm, possibly talking about a permanent relationship?"

Kristi smiled and took a deep breath.

"Never mind," Susan hastily said. "I think I already know."

"It's okay," Kristi replied. "We're praying to see what God has planned for us."

The petite blond leaned closer. "We will be praying God answers soon. Goodness, how exciting."

Exhilaration soared through Kristi's spirit. She didn't want to build false hopes about a life with Jack, but the thoughts lingered with her—teasing and yet promising hope.

"What about his brother?" Kristi asked. "Do you think the situation will someday be resolved?"

Susan shook her head and glanced at the pool where one of the girls complained that another had cheated in their game. After settling the disagreement, she gave Kristi her attention. "Rand does not know the Lord, and he is in denial about Cassidy and other problems in his marriage. It's a sad set of circumstances."

"Especially for two brothers who have only each other in this world," Kristi added. "More items for prayer."

The men emerged from the house and suggested everyone prepare themselves for the evening's activities. Jack quickly stepped to Kristi's side and rested his hand on her shoulder. She adored his touch, his friends, and everything about him. It must be love. She prayed the other problems in his life could be worked out as easily.

Her mom and dad took an instant liking to the five red-headed daughters of Tom and Susan Manning. Country Charm opened its doors in true Texas hospitality, providing fun for everyone long after sunset. Harry could barely contain his excitement with all of the attention, and Keifer, the wagon driver, sang his heart out.

At the close of the evening, Kristi bid her good-byes to the sweet family from Virginia and wished them a safe trip home. Susan and she exchanged telephone numbers and E-mail addresses to keep in touch. Kristi had to smile; her new friend wanted to be one of the first ones to "hear" about Jack and Kristi's prayers.

૨૭

More than a week passed with Jack eagerly anticipating each new day. He wanted to hire an instructor for riding lessons when many people in the community expressed interest. By having someone else deal directly with students, any future repercussion with adverse publicity could be avoided, but he needed to take care of any potential problems first.

Jack took it upon himself to contact Pastor Greg Johnston at Brenham Community Church to first inform him about the circumstances in New York and then to initiate a transfer of membership from Jack's former church to Brenham. The two men met at the church office before a Sunday morning service. Jack carefully explained the entire ordeal surrounding Rand and Cassidy.

"I understand if you need to do some research, and I will gladly meet with the deacons to discuss any of my past," Jack offered. "In fact, I will do whatever you feel necessary to stop any gossip. It's only a matter of time before the papers pick up the story, and I want to be prepared to fight if necessary."

Pastor Greg listened intently. "Jack, I highly respect your coming to me with your concerns. If this was all up to me, I'd say forget the past and welcome your membership into the church, but you and I know people. Even Christian people can be downright ugly. At this point, let me look into the matter. When I get it all compiled, let's talk and possibly set up a deacon's meeting."

"Good." He handed the pastor a folded sheet of paper. "Here's the web site containing the copies of newspaper articles during the arrest and trail. Also, I've jotted down the name and phone number of the law firm that handled my case. They can provide you with all the legal transcripts and references in my behalf. The name and contact information for my previous pastor is there, too. And I've included the name of the correctional institution and its director."

"Whew, you're thorough," Greg replied. "Thanks, I'll be able to take care of this in short order." He took a quick glimpse at the clock on his desk. "Let's go to the Lord in prayer for guidance, and then I've got a sermon to preach."

Jack felt relieved in unloading his doubts to the respected young pastor. He needed to know the church and community supported him down the tough road sure to follow. He didn't want to be pessimistic, but God's Word said to be ready in season and out of season.

sixteen

On Thursday of the following week, Pastor Greg Johnston paid a visit to Bedouin Stables. Since he hadn't visited the horse ranch before, Jack gave him a complete tour of his operation.

"I'm really impressed," Greg said, as they each drank a bottle of cold water in Jack's office. "I had no idea about the history behind Arabian horses, and all this right here in Brenham. The folks here need to know what a great facility you have here."

Jack grinned. There was nothing he liked better than talking about his horse ranch. "After things are resolved, I'd like to invite the youth group out for a tour."

"Wonderful, which brings me to my initial reason for stopping by today. I believe I have gathered all the information needed to call a deacon's meeting, but I still wonder if it's necessary. Seriously, Jack, you are an innocent man, proved so in a court of law."

"Yes, but I was charged, arrested, and sent to jail for assaulting my niece. The accusation alone may cause some good parents to question allowing their kids to come here or be around me."

Greg nodded and rubbed his chin thoughtfully. "I understand, and in your shoes, I'd take the same precautions. How does Sunday evening around five-thirty sound for a meeting?"

Jack agreed, and the two men shook hands. Informing the leaders of Brenham Community Church of his past wouldn't stop people from having skeptical feelings, but if these good men already knew the circumstances, then he'd done his best.

❧

Two weeks had gone by since the deacons, Pastor Greg, and Jack had met to discuss his involvement in the church and the pastor's report about New York. The men voted unanimously both to support Jack and to keep the information private unless a critical situation arose.

Jack engrossed himself in his work and in teaching Kristi how to ride.

"Sit just a little bit straighter. Good girl. Now, loosen those reins." Jack walked around Rosie, carefully assessing Kristi's posture atop the Arabian mare.

This late Saturday afternoon marked their second lesson. They'd talked of postponing it since Labor Day weekend involved a ton of activities, but Kristi didn't want to halt any progress. Since she'd decided to learn to ride properly and cure her fear of horses, it seemed best to continue on a regular basis. Kristi took a deep breath and tried to recall every instruction Jack had given her.

"You can smile, sunshine." He laughed. "You're not getting a grade on this."

"I know," she said, raising her chin, "but I want to make a good impression on my teacher."

"Bribe me," he said. "I am fallible." But when she wrinkled her nose at him, he added, "I was thinking more in terms of a kiss."

Kristi leaned from the saddle and lightly touched his lips with hers.

"Think I'll saddle Desert Wind and join you," he said in a dangerously low voice. "I wouldn't want you bribing anyone else."

They planned to join her parents for dinner at the Country Charm once the guests checked in and were settled. Her dad had insisted upon cooking, so Jack had offered to help. Kristi and her mother had learned the men intended to serve barbecued chicken, tossed salad, baked potatoes, fresh sourdough bread, and homemade vanilla ice cream. It sounded delicious to Kristi and already her stomach rumbled.

An hour later, Jack and Kristi finished their lesson and led the horses into the barn to properly groom them—another one of Jack's scheduled chores for his pupil. She relished every minute of it. Granted, he insisted his horses were ridden and groomed according to precise instructions, but his guidelines came from pride and a great love of the purebreds, and she had begun to feel a similar affection for the horse, along with a growing love for Jack.

During the week their jobs kept them busy, and often they only found time for a few minutes on the phone in the evenings. She always anticipated the weekends when they busied themselves with friends, church activities, and her parents.

Along with their deepening relationship, they found it necessary to establish boundaries in their dating life. They asked her parents to keep them accountable, not just in the physical realm but in their spiritual life, too. She no longer cooked for Jack at his home, but rather invited him to the bed and breakfast where her parents gave them appropriate privacy. She and Jack decided it best if Kristi did not swim alone with him. It invited too much temptation. Above all else, they desired a God-honoring relationship. It proved difficult, but they were convinced that His ways were always the best.

They didn't speak of love. She couldn't bring herself to tell him the depth of her feelings until they both felt God had blessed a life-long commitment between them. Kristi also sensed Jack needed to make amends with his brother.

"Do you mind if I check the messages in my office before I walk you to your car?" Jack asked after they put Rosie and Desert Wind in their stalls.

"No, of course not."

They entered the office in the barn and saw a light flashing on his answering machine. Jack reached over his desk and punched the play button.

"Hi, Jack." He paled and immediately stiffened at the sound of the male voice. "It's been almost two years since I've seen you."

"Oh, no," Jack groaned. "It's Rand."

She slipped her hand into his and leaned on his shoulder.

"I've thought about calling you for some time now, but you know me, I have a company to run. It's not over, yet, brother. We have a lot of unfinished business. Why don't you give me a call at the office?"

The phone clicked, and she stared up into his face. Jack's brows knitted together, and he squeezed her hand firmly. "What do you think?" she whispered.

He shrugged. "Rand didn't sound hostile, but he didn't sound friendly, either."

"Are you going to call him back?"

"Possibly. I imagine he wanted me to call him at the office due to his separation from Lena." Jack seemed to be thinking out loud. He turned and kissed her forehead, which still rested on his shoulder. With a smile, he touched her nose. "Can't phone him until Tuesday with the holiday on Monday," he said. "And it wouldn't hurt to contact my lawyer, Tom, and Pastor Greg before placing the call."

"Anything I can do besides pray?"

"Nope," he said lightly. "I'm ready for whatever Rand has in mind 'cause God is in control." He appeared to be in deep thought, then smiled. "For now, let's get you home so I can shower for dinner." He pulled her around to face him. "Look, we knew this was coming. It will not ruin our weekend."

She nodded, and he held her close. They'd talked about Rand—what he could and might try to do—but until now she'd simply put it out of her mind. Today, she heard a voice with a name. It sounded eerie. Peering into Jack's face, the face of the man she loved, she longed to see him free from pain. *Oh, God,* she inwardly prayed, *speak to Rand's heart; remove his desire for vengeance.*

❧

The Labor Day weekend had been filled with a huge parade and an enormous amount of local activities. Jack and Kristi attended every event possible, even more than they'd originally planned. She knew why and welcomed the distraction. Neither wanted to consider what the next week held. Unfortunately, she had a two-day business meeting in Austin on Tuesday and Wednesday and would not return until nightfall of the second day. Jack indicated he'd phone her as soon as he spoke to his brother, if and when his lawyer advised him to contact Rand.

❧

On Tuesday afternoon, Jack picked up the phone to make the call. Neither his lawyer, Pastor Greg, nor Tom could give him a good reason not to speak with his brother. He'd talked to Kristi, and they'd prayed together for understanding and for neither man to lose his temper.

Taking a ragged breath, Jack punched in the numbers. Odd, he still remembered them. The phone rang twice before his brother answered.

"Rand Frazier here."

Always the business man, he thought grimly. "It's Jack," he said simply. "You asked me to give you a call."

"Well, how's the jailbird doing?" His brother's voice rang with a mixture of bitterness and sarcasm.

"If this is your attitude, I have nothing to say to you," Jack replied.

"These months haven't changed a thing."

Jack detected a slurring of words. Rand had been known to drink a little socially, but at two o'clock in the afternoon? "Have you been drinking?"

"Who are you to question what I'm doing or not doing?" Rand's voice rose.

"Your brother," Jack replied, amazed at his own control.

"My caring little brother who still hides behind a screen of so-called faith to cover up his morals?"

Instead of anger, Jack felt pity for the man on the opposite end of the phone. "Yes, I believe in God, and the evidence proved me innocent."

Rand chuckled. "You, Lena, and Cassidy are in a class all of your own."

"What do you mean?" Jack asked softly.

"Doesn't matter. I just wondered how you were doing."

He wet his lips and searched his mind for a clue as to why Rand had really called. His ramblings didn't make sense. "Why don't you call me when you're thinking more clearly?"

"You mean when I'm not drinking?" he asked, one word drifting into another.

"Yes. Maybe then you can tell me what is really bothering you because right now you don't make sense."

Rand muttered something and hung up the phone. Jack shook his head. He knew his brother well enough to recognize uncharacteristic behavior. Rand drinking in the middle of the day? And why did he put his wife, daughter, and Jack in the same niche? It didn't sound like his level-headed brother at all. Tom hadn't mentioned anything about alcohol abuse, only the separation from Lena. Could this be a cry for help?

Jack rested his head in his hands. He didn't know whether to forget about Rand and go about his business or try to locate the source of his problem. Lifting his head, Jack realized Tom might be able to talk with his brother.

A few moments later after phoning Tom, Jack rose from his desk. Tom seemed just as confused, but he promised to give a Rand a call and fly to New York if needed.

Jack didn't know what to make of the situation. If anything, his older brother had always prided himself in being in control to a fault.

On Wednesday afternoon Jack drove to the bed and breakfast

to meet Kristi, who had arrived home earlier than expected from her two-day business trip. She'd changed into shorts and a T-shirt.

"Let's take a walk," she suggested after he hugged her. "I know just the perfect spot at the back of the property."

"The fishing hole?" Jack asked, linking his fingers into hers. He was so very glad to see her.

"No. It's a little farther down, rather secluded, and very pretty." She grinned and stared up at him with her huge brown eyes. "It's the same place Mom and Dad go when they need time away together."

"Sounds good. I'm stressed to the max."

The two walked out the back door, taking a familiar trail beyond the pecan orchard. They veered to the left away from the fishing area through tall grass. A path led toward a different section of the creek. Beneath a canopy of moss-covered trees and in the cooler temperatures of the shaded bank, Jack and Kristi sat on a log and listened to the chorus of singing insects and birds.

"Peaceful," he remarked, closing his eyes and letting nature soothe his raging spirit. "I feel better already."

"Thought you would," she whispered. "This is definitely God's sanctuary. Dad used to come here as a little boy and bring an old hound with him. Now, he and Mom have Harry tag alongside them." She pointed to the other side of the creek bank. "Over there I've seen deer tracks, but they don't usually come out in the open."

He tugged on her waist and drew her closer to him. "We have a knack of finding the best places to get away from it all. Remember the old stone bridge off the dirt road on the way to town?" When she nodded, he continued. "Since it's starting to get a little cooler in the evenings, we ought to consider a picnic under those trees."

She agreed and yawned, then leaned her head on his shoulder.

"Excuse me, the last few days have worn me out."

"My poor baby," he whispered. "What did those conferees do to you?"

"Night owl sessions," she replied, snuggling against him. "I never saw so many people excited about an investment portfolio."

He laughed and kissed her nose. "What do you have tomorrow?"

"Day-long session in Brenham."

"Looks like I should get you back home. Can't have the instructor falling asleep on the job."

"I'll be just fine," she claimed. "I want to sit here beside you with no worries or cares."

He felt a surge of protective emotions rise in him. He didn't want his Kristi to face any problems or concerns. He wanted to nurture and take care of her for as long as God allowed. It had never occurred to him until that moment how much he loved this woman. She had become as much a part of his life as living and breathing. Only God ruled above his feelings for her.

And then he knew; God intended for Kristi Franklin to always be a part of his life, but he couldn't reveal all of his inner thoughts now. The business with Rand had to be settled first. Yet, some things needed to be said.

Jack tilted her chin to deliver a kiss to her delicious plum lips. Already, shadows of twilight settled around them, and he wondered how long they'd allowed nature's setting to lull them into oblivion.

He threaded his fingers through her rich, cocoa hair, cherishing its silky softness and inhaling its sweet fragrance. Her very presence blended with the woodsy scent showering about them. "Kristi," he began, so quietly as not to break the spell of the moment.

"Hmm," she responded dreamily.

"I love you."

seventeen

Kristi quickly turned to meet his gaze. She touched his cheek, then traced the dimple she'd grown to treasure. "Oh, Jack, it seems like I've waited forever to hear those words, and I do love you," she murmured.

He kissed her again, silently assuring himself that her lips never felt softer or tasted sweeter. He vowed to never love another as he loved her. "Sunshine, I don't know what the future holds for us, and I'm afraid to speculate."

"Whatever it is, I'm right here beside you. I've thought about how wonderful it would be for Rand to have a change of heart, and I've considered the worst. It doesn't matter; my place is with you."

He lifted her chin and stared into those dark pools—the doorway to her heart. "And you're sure?"

"Without a doubt."

He hesitated. Had she really thought through the worst of circumstances, the way people could stare and whisper behind her back? "And what if this thing destroyed your career, your credibility with those who respect you?"

She smiled up at him. "Guess I could always clean out horse stalls."

He pulled her close, desiring nothing but happiness for Kristi, but he knew how quickly things could change from beautiful to devastating. Jack had seen the ugliness of people when provoked at the mention of child abuse, and given the same scenario with someone he loved, he'd react the same way. In many ways, he refused to blame Rand, another reason why he regretted the severed relationship between himself and his brother.

Oh, Lord, am I asking too much of this woman? Am I asking too much of You?

≥∂

Weeks passed and Jack found out little about his brother except he denied the drinking to Tom and referred to Jack as a liar. Rand and Lena were in the midst of counseling, but none of their issues had been resolved. Jack didn't ask Tom about the problems in his brother's marriage; he'd seen it coming for years. They were two people who had run in the opposite direction for so long that they finally collided. They were strangers in the middle of a lifelong commitment. Their marital life needed God as a foundation, not the profits from Rand's business.

Jack watched the days speed by. The weather cooled slightly in the mornings and late evenings to what he once called summer, not Indian summer. The Arabian horses from Egypt responded well to his training, and Fleming Donaldson paid a visit. Jack's life flowed easily, almost too easily.

Every time he said good-bye to Kristi, it gripped a bit of his heart. He didn't want to wait until Christmas to propose marriage. Jack wanted Kristi with him now, as his wife, yet he must protect her from Rand's retaliation. Logic told him he should wait longer in case the newspapers got wind of a story or his brother decided to exploit him. But how long? Sometimes he questioned whether or not he trusted God to see him through.

Early in November, he drove to Austin on a mission. Not a single newspaper reporter had snooped around his place, and Rand had not made any more calls. Jack loved Kristi, and he wanted her with him for the rest of his life. Perhaps the nightmare had finally ended. He decided to propose during the Thanksgiving holiday, and the diamond he desired for her should reflect his unwavering love for her. He sensed more than mere nervousness and excitement with the prospect of asking Kristi to be his wife. Every engagement ring he examined looked perfect until his eyes caught the sparkle of another. Then he found the most stunning of them all.

ॐ

"Do you have plans for Thanksgiving?" Jack asked Kristi a week after he'd made his purchase. His secret made him feel like a little boy with a bag of chocolate candy. They strolled hand in hand through the barns after her riding lesson.

"Not really. I have nothing on my calendar from Wednesday on through the weekend," she replied.

He stopped to lock the tack room and toss a piece of trash into a waste barrel. "Would you like to spend Friday in Houston, take in a museum, see a movie, attempt ice-skating at the Galleria, and have dinner?" He glanced at her for a reaction.

"Definitely." She smiled into his slate gray eyes, warm and full of love. "Everything will be crazy with shoppers, but I can handle the crowds if you don't mind."

"Good," he whispered. "Seems like all I ever do for you is saddle Rosie and dial your phone number."

She laughed. "I'm not complaining. In fact, I'm happy just being with you."

"You're simply brainwashed. My best girl needs spoiling, and I'm afraid I take advantage of you." Jack's attention suddenly focused at the entrance of the barn where two men entered. "Afternoon, can I help you?" he asked good-naturedly.

"Probably so," replied the younger of the two, dressed in jeans and a dirty T-shirt. His mousy brown hair lay about his shoulders in oily ringlets.

Kristi noticed his camera, an expensive one, dangling from his shoulder. She'd never seen either of them before, and a chilling suspicion crept over her.

"We're looking for Jack Frazier," the same man continued with a half grin. "Could he possibly be you?"

She waited for Jack to stiffen or squeeze her hand, but instead, he remained calm.

"Might be," Jack replied casually. "You know, around here a man introduces himself before making assumptions." His steely gaze bore through the unkempt man.

"We're not from around here," the other man said. "Not up on our social skills." He looked older and sported a day-old beard. His shirt gaped open across his wide stomach, revealing two popped buttons. "Of course, we've stopped by before, but Mr. Frazier has never been available. You are him, aren't you?"

Jack swallowed and his face tensed slightly. "Yes, so what do you want?"

Instantly the younger man snapped a picture, then another. "Our readers will want to know where you're living and what you're doing." He turned to Kristi. "Miss, looks to me like you and Frazier are pretty chummy. Do you have any idea about his background?"

Before she could reply, Jack stepped forward. "Get off my property," he ordered. When the younger man lifted his camera to take a third shot, Jack reached to snatch it, but the man pulled the equipment beyond his grasp.

"Let's go," the older man quipped, grabbing the greasy-haired man's arm. "We've got our story and our pictures."

The two men hurried from the barn and into a late model station wagon, caked in dirt and hosting chipped green paint and a dented front fender. The older man wasted no time in putting the aging vehicle into gear and speeding off down the road.

Jack watched them leave, his jaw set angrily. He glanced at Kristi, then back at the car escaping toward Brenham. "Are you all right?" he asked and wrapped his arm around her waist.

"Yes, I'm fine," she whispered. "They were so coarse, so disgusting. I wonder who they represent, and who would want to read anything the likes of those two wrote?"

"Who knows?" he replied. "But a good reporter is a professional, and those guys were losers."

They gazed down the empty road a few moments longer. "What do you think will happen now?" she asked, while a feeling of dread twisted in her stomach.

Jack shook his head. "Oh," he began, then hugged her tighter to him. "Whatever publication those two work for will run an article—complete with photos—then others will get nosy." He wet his lips and peered into her face. "Can you really handle this?"

"Yes, sir. I'm prayed up and ready." Kristi hoped she sounded optimistic. Truth is, the two men had frightened her, but Jack must see that she supported him in whatever lay ahead.

The more she thought about the two men, the more her temper simmered near the boiling point. She couldn't imagine someone making a living from another man's misery. How debase and vile!

Her thoughts shifted to Rand, and she trembled. Why couldn't people leave Jack alone? Hadn't he been through enough over the past two years?

"You're shaking," he said softly.

"I'm furious," she replied, avoiding eye contact.

He rubbed her shoulders and sighed. "Anger doesn't solve a thing, honey. It only eats a hole through your heart and soul."

She waited to reply in an effort to gain control of her raging emotions. "I know what you're saying is true, but this is all so unfair. You're an innocent man."

"Right, and there lies the answer. How does God want us to react? Who are we to cast stones? I don't mean to preach, sunshine. It's just that we've got to look at this through God's eyes."

"Not me," she admitted. "I want to tear them apart with my bare hands."

"Honey."

His soft chiding eased the heavy burden on her mind. "I'm sorry. Let's pray together, okay?"

"Best idea yet, and I'm going to call Pastor Greg." His voice lifted in confidence, and she felt ashamed of her outburst.

"I'll do better," she promised. "I simply have to trust God through this and give Him all of my doubts."

☙

A week later, Carlos reluctantly brought Jack a copy of a national tabloid. Inside the covers, he found his and Kristi's picture splashed across a quarter page, along with an article rehashing the New York incident.

"I'm sorry," the head trainer said, peering anxiously into Jack's face. "Ever since you told me what happened in New York, I've tried to watch for problems."

"It's not your fault," he replied. "I couldn't stop them either." Jack smiled in hopes of calming his friend. "And you're my head trainer, not my bodyguard." He chuckled, and Carlos relaxed. The trainer stood no taller than Jack and just as slender. "I'm all right. Between you, good friends, Pastor Greg, and most importantly, God, I'm doing fine."

"Just wanted you to know I'm sorry," Carlos added.

"No problem, just keep me in your prayers."

Once Carlos left him alone, he thumbed through the paper. In his opinion, the publication didn't look like appropriate reading for good, Christian people. He read through the claims, feeling fury wash over him as though he'd just been arrested. The writer even made his relationship with Kristi look sordid. Taking a deep breath, he asked for God to be glorified in whatever happened.

Luckily, the tabloid had a reputation for printing less than the truth. Thinking about Kristi's engagement ring atop his dresser, Jack wondered if he'd made a mistake. His precious lady didn't deserve any of this.

The week before Thanksgiving, Kristi covered the management duties of the bed and breakfast while her parents attended a community dinner. She sat curled up with Harry in the living room and viewed an old black-and-white Western. At the precise moment when the bad guys had the fair-haired sheriff cornered, the phone rang. Pressing the mute button on the remote, she answered the call.

"Good evening, Country Charm."

"I'd like to make a reservation," a man said.

Kristi scrambled for the computer and pressed the keys to bring up Country Charm's availability. "Yes, sir, when do you need a room?"

"This coming Wednesday."

"And what kind of accommodations do you need?"

"Only myself, for one night."

Kristi punched in the necessary data to block off the room. Luckily they still had rooms. "Your name please?"

"Rand Frazier."

Her fingers froze on the keyboard. Her first inclination was to refuse him a room, but she'd already booked his reservation. "We aren't set up for business meetings, and our rooms aren't equipped with modems," she said, hearing her voice quiver.

"It doesn't matter. I won't be there long."

"But. . ."

"Here is my credit card information. And according to your web page, I can arrive mid-afternoon?"

"Yes, sir," she managed. Kristi couldn't bring herself to thank Rand for the business. Rather, she wanted to tell him he didn't need to set foot any where near Brenham.

"Aren't you located a few miles from Bedouin Stables?"

She gritted her teeth. "It's nearby, but I believe the facilities may be closed during the Thanksgiving holiday."

"No matter."

Rand said a cordial good-bye and hung up, causing Kristi to feel something between desperate and frightened. She picked up the phone to call Jack but changed her mind. Her first thoughts should be on God and prayerfully seeking His guidance and comfort. Again, as in several times over the past weeks, she wished she and Jack were married. Sometimes, she felt as though her hands were tied in helping him. At least if they were husband and wife, he could confide in her. He often gave her the impression he thought he must act brave and courageous for her benefit—as though she needed protection.

She stood and paced the room. First Rand's call, then the disgusting tabloid article, and now his brother's visit. *Oh, God, help me to stand beside Jack with the attitude You desire of me. I'm scared for him. I know it's selfish, but I'm also scared for us.*

eighteen

Staring at the slow drizzle on his kitchen window, Jack realized the weather echoed his mood. He traced a raindrop slipping down the outer pane, not knowing where it might fall. The water's uncertain destination reminded him of his unrest. Only God knew where he and Rand would stand at the close of the day. Jack's comfort lay in that God knew him, He had the situation under control, and He would not leave His child alone.

Thanksgiving eve, a time to reflect over the year's blessings and to gather around loved ones. Rand had never cared for family affairs. He claimed holidays made him uncomfortable, and as soon as the food disappeared, he escaped to the solitude of his high-rise office until the festivities ended. His choice to spend Thanksgiving away from home didn't surprise Jack.

Fortunately, good people were praying. Rick had stopped by earlier to encourage him, and Paula had sent chocolate fudge muffins. Pastor Greg phoned to check on him, and a deacon offered lunch. Jack had refrained from eating. His stomach knotted at the thought of food.

He thought of Kristi's earlier phone call. She'd blamed herself for Rand's visit, an idea which Jack promptly refuted. Rand would have showed up at Bedouin Stables whether he had a room booked at the Country Charm or not. Jack let out a frustrated sigh. What a way to begin his proposal weekend. Depending upon the outcome, there might not be a marriage proposal on Saturday morning at all.

I've got to be hopeful, he told himself. *Good things can come out of this.*

❧

By late afternoon, the rain stopped, and the weather dipped into the forties. Welcoming the crisper temperatures, Kristi momentarily pushed Rand's arrival from her mind. She helped her mother roll out pie dough and bake corn bread for the turkey dressing. Guests were booked at the bed and breakfast for the night. A huge breakfast buffet was planned to top their morning, but Country Charm would be closed on Thanksgiving.

Her mother chatted on about the following day's dinner and all the friends and family scheduled to spend the holiday with them. Kristi tried to respond enthusiastically, but depression kept clouding her feelings.

The doorbell rang, and Kristi's gaze darted toward the front of the house. Although none of the other guests had arrived, she suspected Rand might check in early.

"I'll get it," her mother said, wiping her hands on a towel and whisking off her apron.

While she hurried to answer the door, Kristi stole a glimpse at the car parked outside. She scrutinized the vehicle—white, exclusive, and definitely rented. Kristi closed her eyes to form some resemblance of a prayer. Instead bile rose in her throat, and she fought the sensation to be sick.

I'm such a good, trusting Christian, she scolded herself. *Just where is my faith?*

While Kristi measured syrup for pecan pies, her mother entered the kitchen.

"It's him. He has the same gray eyes and light hair," she whispered. "He said he has an errand to run and might be gone until late." Her mother's hazel gaze looked troubled. "I feel as though I've betrayed Jack by having his brother spend the night."

"You!" Kristi replied with an exasperated sigh. "I took the reservation." She picked up the phone and punched in Jack's number and waited for him to answer. "He's here," she said a moment later after hearing the familiar voice.

"Okay. I'm waiting. Did you talk to him?" Jack asked.

"No, I haven't even seen him." She glanced out the window at his car. "Oh, Jack," she managed. "I'd like to. . .like to—"

"What does my feisty lady want to do?"

"Let the air out of his tires, drain his radiator, pull out a few wires," she blurted. "I know I'm terrible, but that is exactly how I feel."

He chuckled. "Sure glad you're on my side."

"I'm sorry. This is the time I'm supposed to be offering you support, and instead I'm whining." She took a deep breath. "I will do better. You just hang up the phone, and I'll be praying until I hear from you."

" 'Atta girl. I love you."

"I love you." Kristi replaced the phone and smiled up at her mother. "Sure wish my temper didn't get the best of me. I'm ashamed of myself."

"God knows your heart," her mother said, "and He knows how much you love Jack." The front door shut and she jumped. "Let's both talk to Him awhile."

❧

Pouring himself a fresh cup of black coffee—and definitely not decaf, Jack waited in his barn office for Rand. He felt more comfortable among the familiar sights and smells of his horses than in the house listening to the lonesome sound of a ticking clock.

A light rap sounded at the door. Jack knew it had to be Rand. Stiffening, he silently accepted whatever transpired with his brother. "Yes?"

"Rand Frazier here to see you," Carlos called.

"Send him in." He wanted to appear casual, no big deal. Setting his coffee cup on the desk, he started down the hall to the door.

Jack watched the brass knob turn and click.

ъ

"You're gonna wear a hole in the floor," her mother accused as Kristi paced back and forth across the kitchen, palming the rolling pin in her hand. "And Rand's been gone but a few minutes. He's barely had time to drive down the road."

"Oh, Mom, how will I make it until Jack calls? I wish I could be there with him."

"Honey, this is between Jack and Rand. We have to believe in God's provision."

Kristi stood still. "Some times, such as right now, I think I haven't progressed at all in my relationship with the Lord. I know I should trust Him to work out Jack and Rand's differences, but then those doubts creep in again."

"Honey, it's all our journey of faith," her mother said, pouring pumpkin pie mixture into two crusts. She set the bowl on the counter. "None of us will ever feel perfectly satisfied with how we handle the problems in our lives, but with God's help, we'll do better through each adversity."

Kristi smiled. "How did you become so wise?"

Her mother laughed. "By trying to keep up with you."

ъ

"You look good," Rand said, shaking Jack's hand at the doorway. "Thanks for letting me see you today."

Jack stared into his brother's eyes and saw no malice or contempt. He gripped Rand's hand firmly. "I'm glad you came. Seems like you're always on my mind." Moving away from the door, he gestured down the office hallway. "Come on in; I have a fresh pot of coffee made."

"Are you still brewing it so strong it takes your breath away?"

Jack appreciated Rand's attempt at humor. "Not quite." He smiled. "I've changed brands and taken a few tips from some friends, in fact, the same people who own the bed and breakfast where you're staying."

Rand nodded. "Mrs. Davenport was very cordial."

He noticed his brother still dressed to perfection in a starched designer shirt and dark, exquisitely tailored slacks. Neither man said a word while Jack poured Rand's coffee and offered a packet of sugar and a plastic spoon. Taking both, Rand stirred the hot liquid while looking about the room. He commented on Jack's apparent organization, but he appeared nervous.

"Have a seat," Jack urged, "and tell me what brings you here." He waited until his brother eased into a chair across from his desk. Jack preferred the small seating area on the adjacent side, but he allowed Rand to set the pace. Again silence reigned around them.

Rand took a sip of coffee. "I don't know where to begin." When Jack refused to comment, he continued. "You're not going to make this easy for me, are you?"

He cleared his throat. "Our past conversations weren't the most pleasant."

"My fault. . .so I'll speak my piece. Jack, I came here to apologize. I've been wrong, spiteful—all the things I never wanted to be. I was instrumental in sending you to jail and made sure you stayed there. I deliberately tried to destroy your business by leaking private information to newspapers and your friends. Most of all, I'm guilty of letting you parent my daughters rather taking the responsibility myself." He took a labored breath. "I wanted to punish you when things didn't turn out like I desired."

Jack's mind echoed with Rand's words. He felt his eyes dampen, and he hastily blinked away the threat of tears. In his bewilderment, he nearly tipped over his cup. "Why now?" he asked.

Rand chewed on his lip, and Jack saw he bordered on emotionally falling apart. Never had he seen his brother display sentiment, even at the trial. He had remained stoic, calculating, and cold.

"Three weeks and four days ago, I accepted Jesus Christ as my Lord and Savior. . .and so did Cassidy. You see, she's in a rehabilitation center, a Christian facility." He took another deep breath and a gulp of coffee. "It's probably no surprise to you she went deeper and deeper into the drug world until she overdosed. Lena couldn't handle it, so she dumped it in my lap. That was the day I phoned you, drunk. Even then, I couldn't bring myself to ask for help. I just blamed you for my miserable life."

He shook his head. "Uncle Jack wasn't at my beck and call to pick up the pieces, and I had to face reality myself. Anyway, I searched out a hospital setting based on its excellent reputation, only to find the center advertised itself as Christian based." Stands of gray entwined with yellow framed Rand's face, and many lines etched the corners of his eyes.

"One Sunday, Cassidy's doctor suggested I attend a worship service with her. While listening to the minister, it occurred to me you had told me the same things about God and His Son, Jesus, for years, but I just simply ignored it. Frankly, I believed you used religion as a crutch—I thought you were jealous of my success and swore allegiance to some God to mask your inferior feelings." He paused, and Jack saw how difficult the words came to Rand.

"My business of making money took priority over my most important asset—my family. Cassidy seemed to hear it for the first time, too. We both accepted the Lord's invitation at the close of the sermon."

"Rand," Jack managed. Suddenly all the misery of the past two years held clarity and meaning. He realized everything had happened to bring his brother to the Lord.

He started to speak, but Rand lifted his hand. "I. . .I need to finish. Cassidy confessed to me your innocence. She knew how much you loved her and how telling me about the drug transaction was for her own good." He shifted in the chair.

"So, I came to not only ask you to forgive me, but to deliver this." He pulled an envelope from his shirt pocket and handed it to Jack. "Cassidy isn't permitted to leave the facility yet, but she asked me to deliver this letter."

Solemnly, Jack took the envelope, not sure if he should read it now or later.

"Go ahead," Rand urged. "It's important to me. . .to Cassidy."

He slipped his forefinger beneath the sealed portion and slowly lifted the flap, making sure not to tear any of it. His mind felt numb, and he trembled much like the day when he'd rededicated his life to Jesus. His gaze fell to the familiar handwriting:

Dear Uncle Jack,

I hope you will read this and understand how sorry I am for all the horrible things I have done to you. I lied and accused you of something terrible to save myself. You loved me when my parents ignored me. You loved me when I didn't deserve it. Now, I see how Jesus lived in you, and I pray someday, someone will see Him in my life, too.

I know my dad has explained what has been going on in his life and mine; I'm just so sorry it all came about because of my lies and deceit. I don't know why I never listened to you or Carla talk about a relationship with the Lord. Guess my way looked like the best. Please forgive me. I know I can't change any of the awful things that happened to you or give you back the days spent in jail, but I am truly sorry. I love you, Uncle Jack, and I only wish I could be there in person to say the things in my heart.

I pray you and my dad can be brothers again, real brothers this time. I hope you will be able to forgive the awful nightmare I caused.

Love,
Cassidy

Jack folded the letter and neatly tucked it inside the envelope. He stood, his eyes brimming with tears. "Rand, I'm a firm believer a man isn't a man until he can shed tears and say exactly how he feels. I'm sorry for the bitterness I've had for so long. I do love you, brother." He swallowed hard and walked around his desk. "I would gladly spend the rest of my life in jail to have this moment now with you."

In all of his life, Jack had never hugged his brother. Rand had never felt it appropriate, even when their parents died. But those days were gone. They hugged and cried, washing away the many years of misunderstandings and replacing them with hope for the future and the mutual bond of Christ.

nineteen

Kristi's mother refused her help for dinner, especially after she dropped a dozen eggs on the floor and knocked a ten-pound bag of sugar over top of them. After she cleaned up the horrendous, sticky mess, her mother strongly suggested she set the table for Thanksgiving breakfast and leave her culinary inclinations alone until her nerves settled.

With more than a few ruffled feathers, Kristi had rummaged through the oak sideboard for the exact set of china. She sighed and took a quick glimpse at her watch—for nearly the thousandth time. Why hadn't Jack called? The two men had met three hours ago. What happened, and where were they?

She placed a gold fork beside a gold-rimmed china plate. Gingerly, she added a knife and spoon to the other side. Taking a burnt orange cloth napkin, she folded it into a fan and slipped it inside a gold ring. She took a moment to study the napkin rings used at Thanksgiving for more than a decade. A raised etching of praying hands adorned each one. Resting it by the forks, Kristi double-checked to make sure every eating utensil sparkled. Her mother enjoyed serving a formal breakfast, and the meal planned for the following morning would suit a king.

A few moments later, she stood in the doorway of the dining room to get the full effect of the table decorations. Earlier that afternoon, her mother had purchased a cornucopia filled with an assortment of fall flowers as a centerpiece. Kristi loved this room with its antique quilt wall hanging artfully displayed and the mammoth oak sideboard containing new and old sets of dishes. In a small alcove sat a spinning wheel, which had once been a part of this farmhouse. It all looked homey and inviting. She wished her insides felt the same ease.

The phone rang, startling her senses, and she pulled it out of her purple plaid flannel shirt pocket. In her haste, she suddenly forgot how to answer appropriately in case the call related to the bed and breakfast. Her mouth went dry as she attempted to offer a polite greeting.

"Kristi?" a familiar voice asked.

"Oh, Jack, are you all right?" Her voice rattled. "I've been so worried, wondering what was going on."

"Everything is fine, sunshine. Rand and I have been talking, and the time escaped me. I'm sorry for not calling sooner."

She smiled and allowed her body to relax. "So, it's good? You have been able to talk about your problems?"

"That and more. It couldn't be better. Rand and I are heading into Brenham for some dinner. You know, my favorite restaurant, and I think we'll probably stop at Pastor Greg's afterward. Is it okay if we come by the bed and breakfast about nine?"

"Sure, of course," she answered while noting how mellow and peaceful his voice sounded. *Thank You, Lord,* she prayed. "I am really happy for you. Honey, you sound like a different man."

"I am, and so is my brother. It's a long story, but I'll tell you all about it later." The pride in which he said "my brother" gave her goose bumps.

She heard Rand comment about something in the background, and Jack chuckled. "He wants to know if it's safe to drive over, or if you're going to let the air out of his tires?"

Kristi gasped. "You told him about that?"

"No." He laughed heartily. "Rand overheard you before he left this afternoon. He's anxious to meet you."

"I am so embarrassed," she moaned, recalling how silly her

threat must have sounded to a complete stranger. After relaying her apologies to Rand, they said their good-byes.

"Mom, Jack and Rand are actually spending time together and talking out their problems," she shouted into the kitchen.

Kristi danced around the dining room, stopping momentarily to lean over the table and inhale the fresh scent of the flowers. For the second time, she peered out over the china and crystal placed for the next morning's breakfast. It dazzled her, and she laughed aloud.

Her mother stood in the doorway. "What an improvement in your mood," she said with a grin. "One call from Jack and you're swinging from the chandelier. And such exciting news."

"Mom, I could actually feel Jack's happiness over the phone. How perfectly wonderful!" She didn't know how it all happened except that God had definitely intervened to bring the brothers together. She couldn't ask for a more perfect Thanksgiving celebration.

えぁ

Shortly after nine o'clock, Jack pulled his pickup into the driveway of Country Charm. After talking for hours, he and Rand had enjoyed the best of Brenham's home-style cooking and then visited Pastor Greg. With the life-changing decision his brother had made, Jack wanted his pastor to hear the good news. Now, he wanted his brother to meet his Kristi.

"Tell me, little brother, how serious is this between you and Kristi?" Rand asked, as Jack switched off the ignition.

He grinned and curled his fingers around the truck keys. "I plan on asking her to marry me on Saturday."

Rand's eyes widened. "She has to be a brave girl to take you on," he teased. "But she does sound like quite a character. You have no idea what ran through my mind when she burst out with what she wanted to do to my car."

Jack chuckled. "Well. . ." He searched for the right words to describe her. "Kristi is very. . .real. . .alive. . .spunky, like a breath of fresh air." He nodded to emphasize his next statement. "And she is drop-dead gorgeous—plus my best friend."

Rand groaned. "You're definitely in love." He paused, and his tone became serious. "I hope she knows what a prize she has in you. I'm praying Lena and I can recapture our old magic before it's too late. I want to be a husband and father in all aspects of the terms." He reached for the door handle. "It will come. Right now let me be properly introduced to the woman who has tamed my bro."

"I'll be praying for you. By any chance, are you interested in being my best man, providing she says yes?"

"You bet, and thanks."

They exited the vehicle and ambled across the yard to the front door of the bed and breakfast. Jack hadn't known such contentment in a long time and never with his brother. In all of his reflections of the troubles he and Rand experienced, he'd never dreamed God intended to use those bad times for good. But wasn't that like the Master Planner?

Kristi opened the door before Jack's feet reached the top step of the porch. In the soft glow of the outside light beaming from above their heads, he caught a sparkle in her mink brown eyes. The intensity outshone the most exquisite diamond. He fought hard the urge to take her into his arms and kiss her soundly.

Immediately, she extended her hand to Rand. "Hi, I'm Kristi Franklin. It's a pleasure to meet you."

Rand placed his hand over hers and smiled. "So you are the girl who has smitten Jack. You are lovely, although I don't understand what you see in this horseman brother of mine."

"My true qualities," Jack said and kissed Kristi's cheek. "And don't be telling her all of my faults."

"I'm sure they aren't worth mentioning," she added with a light laugh. "Won't you come inside?"

Once the three were seated in the living room, Rick and

Paula entered from the kitchen, both brimming with hospitality. Rick introduced himself to their guest and welcomed him into their home. Jack loved this family, in truth, his second family. They made Rand feel as welcome as they had always done for him. Stealing a side glance at Kristi seated beside him, he winked and gathered her hand into his. Pure joy emitted from his soul.

His thoughts touched on the problems still needing to be worked out with Rand, specifically his brother's marriage. Jack observed him sitting in an overstuffed chair to his right, completely relaxed. Time and prayer would handle those unpleasant situations in their family. Jack held no doubts.

"I have several pies in the kitchen," Paula began. "We'll never eat them all tomorrow, and some are still warm."

"I don't know," Rand said, shaking his head. "We ate a big dinner."

"But you've never eaten Paula's pies," Jack pointed out. "I will take a slice of whatever kind you have extra of."

"Pumpkin?" Paula questioned. When he nodded, she turned to Rand. "And you?"

"I guess the same. At the rate I'm going tonight, I'll be the turkey tomorrow."

"Speaking of Thanksgiving," Rick began. "Rand, you are welcome to share dinner with us. My other four kids and their families will be here, too."

Rand looked amazed. Jack knew his brother wasn't accustomed to Southern social etiquette. "I have a flight out of Houston at one and a date with my daughter, Carla, for the evening, then I'm spending all day Friday with my oldest daughter, Cassidy. But thank you for the invitation. I appreciate it."

"Well, I certainly understand wanting to get back to your family. I'd be chomping at the bit to catch a flight home." Rick turned his attention to Jack. "We will have a great breakfast in the morning. Why don't you join us? I mean, if you two fellas don't have other plans."

"You bet," Jack replied without hesitation. "Thanks."

Paula took pie orders, but Rick declined. He planned to eat heartily the next day. The silver-haired gentleman slipped his arm around his wife's waist, and the couple disappeared to serve the dessert and coffee.

"Do you need help?" Kristi asked, standing.

"No, you enjoy the company. We've got it handled," her dad replied.

"Good people," Rand murmured. "Jack, I'm pleased for you." He patted Harry on the head. The dog had taken an evident liking to the bed-and-breakfast guest. "Kristi," he began. "Thank you for taking such good care of my brother. He's obviously very happy."

She fairly beamed. "Oh, we had a rocky beginning, but once we stopped throwing stones at each other, we got along quite nicely."

"Did you ever sabotage his car?" Rand's gray gaze challenged hers while his lips curved upward.

"No," she replied laughing, her cheeks tinting a little more peach. "But I sure did a lot of other things."

Rick and Paula delivered the pie and coffee and served the others before excusing themselves so the three could talk freely. They ate and talked until several rounds of yawns caused them to declare it a night.

Once Rand mounted the winding staircase to his room, Jack and Kristi stood alone in the foyer. In the muted shadows, he simply wanted to hold Kristi close. The quiet intertwined with the smells of food waiting to be eaten the following day caused him to ache for his own home—shared with Kristi. One day he wanted children who all looked like their dark-eyed mother.

So many things had happened today, and it was too late for

him to share it all with her. He pulled her into his embrace, cherishing her closeness while the intoxicating effect of her perfume played havoc with his mind. He whispered in her ear, "I missed you today."

"And I missed you."

"Absence makes the heart grow fonder," he continued. "Did I quote it right?"

"Perfectly, but it also makes you lonely." She brushed a kiss across his cheek.

He combed his fingers through her thick, brown hair, separating the strands cascading down her back. "Sunshine, Rand's found the Lord."

"An answer to prayer," she softly replied. "Yet I suspected so. He has that certain look about him. True peace."

While they held each other, Jack briefly relayed Rand's recent conversion and his purpose for coming to Texas as well as Cassidy's letter. The details would have to wait.

"Now I know the reason why my world turned upside down the way it did—and just after I'd resigned myself to believing I'd never find out until I reached heaven." He stepped back to view her face and lifted her chin. "You gave me the courage to face life again instead of wallowing in self-pity. Everything you did pointed to the Lord. For that, I love you even more."

"Oh, Jack, not everything," she said with a look of chagrin upon her delicate features.

"Yes," he insisted. "You showed me God delights in all of His children and has a purpose for each one of us."

She hastily blinked her eyes just before he bent to taste her lips. God had been really good to him, and he felt so unworthy of all the blessings—Kristi, Rand, and a great life among people who cared about him. Granted, he knew the news papers would be chasing him for a long while, and the aftermath of the articles might lead others to doubt his credibility, but he had God to see him through.

❧

Promptly at 8:45 the next morning, Jack arrived for Thanksgiving Day breakfast. With the seven guests, Country Charm served a royal meal—festive and warm. Auburn-haired Paula served platter after platter of fruit, muffins, homemade molasses bread, pancakes, three different types of syrup, scrambled eggs, bacon, sausage, hashed brown potatoes, a potato and cheese casserole, oatmeal, and a blueberry cobbler—not to mention the different juices, teas, and assorted flavors of coffee. Good thing dinner had been scheduled for two-thirty because no one would have room any earlier.

Afterward, Jack and Rand took a long walk through the pecan orchard before heading over to Jack's for the rental car. Although their visit had been short, it had erased years of heartache for both of them. They promised to pray for each other and settled on a time to talk each week. Jack wanted to visit Cassidy before Christmas, and hopefully he could spend some time with Lena and Carla. Rand had a difficult road ahead of him with his family, but he wouldn't go through it alone. He now knew the Lord.

twenty

The following day found Kristi and Jack leaning over the upper railing of the three-storied Galleria Mall in Houston, watching the ice-skaters. From toddlers to teens and on to a tenacious white-haired grandmother, all attempted to glide across the ice. Shoppers galore moved from store to store, looking for the best buys of the holiday season while the majority of men looked extremely bored.

Jack and Kristi had spent a good bit of their time people watching. Houston, the home of so many different nationalities, invited everyone to the first official day of Christmas shopping. The entire mall appeared to be wrapped with miles of gold ribbon, and a giant Christmas tree, the height of two shopping floors, glowed with a million twinkling white lights.

"This is my favorite time of the year," Kristi said, glancing about at the brightly colored decorations.

"Mine, too," Jack replied. "I think it's all that peace and goodwill snowing on everyone."

"Here, it's raining, not snowing," she pointed out. "And I believe the temperature is in the mid-seventies."

They laughed, and he gave her waist an affectionate squeeze. "Give me time. I'll get it all down right," he said.

A young girl dressed in red and white and wearing a Santa's cap did a perfect double axel on the ice below them. The crowd clapped as she skated away.

"When was the last time you went ice-skating?" Kristi asked and cringed as a stocky youth sprawled out below them.

"A few years ago, but I'm used to wearing a coat and gloves. Your way looks a little too easy for this cold-weather boy." He grinned and winked. "Do you think you should attempt strapping on a pair of skates with your knack at breaking bones?"

Kristi wrinkled her nose at him. "No problem. My legs are stronger than ever—and so is my foot."

"But what about on ice? Do you want to chance facing Christmas with another cast?" A smile pulled at his lips, and if they hadn't been in public, she'd have begged for a kiss.

"I've been looking forward to this since you mentioned it," she said. "You can't baby me forever."

"Oh, I can try," he whispered, and Kristi's heart fluttered at the sound of his words. "I'll have to be ready to catch you if you fall."

After locking their few packages in a mall locker, they braved themselves onto the ice. To her delight, it didn't take long for them to warm up and skate beautifully together. They wove in and out of children, daring kids, and those who greeted the ice with their backsides. Holiday music gave her more energy and enthusiasm than she thought imaginable. Or maybe the gush of excitement came from her love for Jack.

"Thanks for taking me to the art museum this morning," she managed breathlessly as they skated hand in hand.

"Glad you enjoyed it. I do admit some of it looked like pre-school paintings."

They laughed, for neither had particularly appreciated certain aspects of the art tour. As they recovered from their amusement, Jack lost his balance and released her hand just before he fell. He tried to fake a broken ankle, but she saw through his antics. Still laughing, she helped him to his feet.

"Looks like I'm the one who needed a guardian angel," he said. "And just where were you when my feet flew out from under me?"

"Expecting you to recover," she giggled. Feeling like a

child completely engrossed in fun, Kristi didn't want their time to end.

Afterward they sipped on hot chocolate smothered with a large dollop of whipped cream. Jack insisted upon a chocolate chip cookie, and Kristi nibbled on a peanut butter bar.

"Where do you want to have dinner tonight?" Jack asked, as they browsed through a bookstore, carrying their warm drinks. He picked up a calendar for the upcoming year, one with colorful photos of Arabian horses.

"What? You've just filled me with cocoa and a cookie, and now you're talking dinner?" Kristi said in mock annoyance.

"I don't want you fainting from hunger. Besides, I may need to make reservations."

Kristi shook her head. "No, let's not go to so much bother. We're dressed casually, so why not eat some place we don't have to worry about clothes?"

"Okay," he slowly replied. "I just want today to be special. So what sounds good? Your wish is my command." He bent low with a wave of his hand as though she were royalty.

"You're crazy." She laughed and tapped her chin with her finger. "Do you like Mexican food?"

Jack shrugged, his dimple deepening. "I guess. All I've ever had is the fast-food variety."

Her eyes widened. "Honest? Oh, Jack, you've been deprived of the greatest taste treat imaginable. I'm so sorry I haven't invited you over when Irene brings one of her specialties. She used to cook at a Mexican restaurant in San Antonio, and she is the best. Anyway, I know the perfect place. You'll just love it."

"Sounds good to me. Would you like to take in a movie before then?"

"Sure. You are definitely spoiling me," she said, offering a look that conveyed her gratitude.

His tender gaze held all the love she could ever want to see.

"I like spoiling you," Jack whispered. He replaced the calendar, and she raised a questioning brow. "I've changed my mind. You see, I know this great girl who takes better pictures than these."

"Well," she began slowly. "On Wednesday I received notification from the photo contest, and I received honorable mention. I meant to tell you sooner, but with Rand arriving and all, I forgot."

"Humph, they must have had lousy judges," he said. "Sorry, sunshine, all the more reason why we need to see a great movie. Now, what sounds good to you?"

"Oh, you can pick. All day we've done things for me. It's your turn."

He planted a kiss on her cheek. "Excuse me. I couldn't help myself, but you're too irresistible. About the movie. . .I see a holiday special is showing—a family comedy."

"Perfect," she immediately replied.

Jack glanced at his watch and pulled a piece of paper from his jeans pocket. "I did an online search this morning for what was playing—and the ratings."

She peered over his shoulder as he scanned the list for the movie.

"Found it," he said, "but we'd better hurry if we're going to make it on time. It has a great review."

While they rushed to Jack's truck, Kristi remembered all the times she'd termed a date as a formal dinner with proper theater tickets. Today had been so wonderful, and she wanted to remember every minute of it. How could life get any better?

After the lighthearted movie, Jack drove down Westheimer, looking for Kristi's favorite Mexican restaurant. When they couldn't find it, they had to stop to ask for directions, a chore Jack detested. Sensing his discomfort, she asked a service station attendant for the address.

"I know Austin inside and out," she told him, as he read

through her instructions. "But Houston is another matter."

"Don't placate me," Jack grumbled. "I'm one of those men who thinks asking for directions is a threat to my male ego."

Her lips curved into a smile; she couldn't resist teasing him. "Oh? You have faults? I would never have guessed."

He ignored her and continued driving. "See," he said triumphantly, pointing to the restaurant in question. "I found it."

"Yes, sir," Kristi conceded, "but remember, you followed the directions I got for you."

"You're such a good, humble woman," he said, "but I love you anyway."

"I know," she replied. "We love each other. That's why we put up with each other's quirks."

Jack enjoyed the Mexican food. In fact, he complimented Kristi on her excellent choice. All the while, he thought about the proposal in the morning. While at the bed and breakfast Thanksgiving afternoon, under the sounds of a televised football game, he'd talked to Rick about his plans. Jack had apologized for not getting Rick's consent to marry his daughter before purchasing the ring.

"Jack," Rick had said softly, after making sure Paula and Kristi were not in the room. "Thank you for having the respect for me to ask my permission. Kristi is my baby girl, not of my flesh, but of my heart. I get a special feeling when she calls me Dad because it's never been necessary. I love her, and I want her happy." He paused and his blue eyes moistened. "I can't think of anyone I would welcome more as a son-in-law than you." He chuckled. "Of course, she can be a bit high-spirited at times, but so can her mother. Makes life exciting. . .and a lot of fun."

Jack inwardly smiled when recalling the conversation. He hoped Kristi assumed they had known each other long enough. And the ring. Would she like it? His stomach did a series of flips. It was a good thing he intended to propose only once in his life because his heart couldn't handle any more stress.

Much later as they lingered on the front porch of Country Charm, he considered how he could mention the next day without giving away his eagerness.

"Would you like to ride in the morning?" he asked, wrapping his arms around her in the chilly night air.

"Early?"

He kissed her nose. "No. Sleeping Beauty may not need her sleep, but I do. Is ten-thirty okay?"

"Yes, it's fine. I promised Mom and Dad I'd help them begin unpacking and sorting through the Christmas decorations in the afternoon."

I just pray you will be showing off a diamond and talking wedding plans, he thought. "Good, let me give you one more kiss before I send you off to bed."

"Hmm," she replied dreamily. "How about two?"

৯

Kristi woke after a restful night's sleep at nearly nine o'clock. She'd intended to help Mom and Irene with breakfast and felt a bit ashamed of herself for staying in bed. "Should have set my alarm," she scolded.

Rising, she headed to the shower and thought about the previous day with Jack and smiled. Wonderful, absolutely wonderful. She loved that man more each day. Sometimes, like this morning, she allowed herself to dream about a life with him, as his wife—Mrs. Jack Frazier. Did he ever think about the same things?

A short while later, Kristi pushed back the circular shower curtain and emerged from the claw-foot bathtub. Glancing about her, she recalled Thanksgiving Day and all of the blessings she possessed. Her home with Mom and Dad for starters, even if she did desire a place of her own. Her mother had gone to so much work and effort to decorate Kristi's bath and bedroom. The deep green bathtub stenciled in pink roses and the wallpaper in tiny pink rosebuds and ivy had once been featured in a country decorator magazine along with her bedroom.

With her hair wrapped in a thick, spruce-green towel, she stepped into her bedroom to find her favorite gold sweater and jeans. Sorting through her green armoire stenciled in the same pink roses as her bathtub, she took a moment to appreciate the beauty of the room.

The walnut bed with its huge, lace-carved headboard had been a family heirloom on the Franklin side of her family. Pale pink walls, a window treatment in the same light rose and spruce-green treatment, a white eyelet bed coverlet, and a dried rose swag over the window all added up to beauty. . . and charm. *Like my talented mom,* she told herself. Eyeing the Swedish ivy in need of water that was positioned on an antique plant stand, she returned to the bathroom to tend to it.

She finished drying her hair and decided to wear it down, due to the slightly cooler temperatures predicted for the morning. She hated for her ears to get cold. Applying a light sponging of makeup, mascara, and lipstick, she thought how funny for her to pamper her looks when in no time at all she'd smell like a horse.

After making her bed and snatching up her purse and keys from a cherry marble-topped English washstand, she headed to the kitchen for a quick breakfast before driving over to Jack's.

" 'Morning, Mom. " 'Morning, Irene," she greeted, stopping to give them each a hug.

"Did you have a good time yesterday?" her mother asked, bustling about the kitchen, cleaning up after the guests' breakfast.

"You bet," she replied, pouring a cup of cinnamon-flavored coffee. Peering over the plate of muffins in an attempt to decide which one she wanted, she saw her dad enter from the dining room with an armful of dishes. Kristi nibbled on her lip and rushed to his aid. "I'm so sorry I overslept," she said.

"I should have been up helping."

"No problem," Rick said, his crystal blue eyes sparkling. "You had a big day and another one today."

She turned her startled gaze to his face. "No, I don't. Well, not really. Jack and I are riding at ten-thirty, and this afternoon I'm going to sort through the Christmas decorations with you and Mom."

"Oh," he said quickly. "Sounds big enough to me."

She looked at him, wondering why he thought today would be any different than any other Saturday—chores and catch-up. It must be the holiday and all the preparations for the bed and breakfast. "I can cancel this morning, if you want," she offered. "I wasn't here yesterday, and I'm sure Jack would understand."

"Definitely not," her mother said rather sharply and glared at her dad. "You have plans this morning, and you should keep them. Isn't that right, Rick?"

"Yes, of course," he said without hesitation.

Puzzled, Kristi shook her head. "You two need to slow down a bit," she encouraged. "Enjoy life. Don't you agree, Irene?"

The petite lady simply smiled. "We all need to relax."

Kristi took a swallow of coffee and assisted her dad in clearing the table before she snatched up an apple muffin en route to the back door. "Bye, ya'll. I'll make the ride short and see you about noon."

She heard the three in the kitchen laugh as the door shut behind her. Taking in a breath of cool air, she looked forward to a good ride. The sky seemed incredibly blue this morning. Soft, billowy white clouds indicated a marvelous day and certainly warm temperatures by the afternoon. A flash of her job responsibilities for the next week and a decision on purchasing the duplex in Brenham crossed her mind, but she firmly pushed those issues aside. She promptly declared it Scarlett O'Hara Day and said she would think about those things tomorrow.

twenty-one

Arriving at Bedouin Stables right on schedule, Kristi felt her smile might be permanently etched on her face. The times she got to see Jack every day helped compensate for when her job kept her out of town. As she pulled into his driveway, she remembered tossing his keys in front of his door and forgetting her shoes. Oh, how they had laughed over their first meeting.

And what a change in their relationship—from wanting to put him in his place to wanting him to hold her forever. *I'm a helpless, hopeless, dreamy romantic,* she thought with a laugh.

Walking into the barn, she waived at Carlos and the other trainers who were busy at work. "Hey, guys," she called. "Did you have a good Thanksgiving?"

They all responded positively. "Still stuffed," replied Carlos. "You know how my Aunt Irene cooks, and we have lots of food left over—turkey sandwiches all next week for lunch."

She nodded. "At our house it's casseroles and soup, too." She craned her neck for signs of Jack. "Do you know where he is? We're supposed to go riding." She peered into Rosie's stall and saw she hadn't been saddled. A little confused, she looked to Carlos for possible answers.

He stopped brushing the gray gelding in his care. "Jack asked me to have you meet him in the far pasture. He said you knew where."

"Walk or ride?"

"Walk. Guess he's waiting there for you."

She smiled and thanked him. Taking a peek, she saw Desert Wind wasn't in his stall. What did he plan for her to ride? Moving on through the barn, she strolled toward the far pasture. Kristi knew the site well. She and Jack had picnicked beneath a towering live oak in September. The day had been humid and hot, and later it clouded up and stormed. A few times, he'd mentioned taking pictures in the secluded setting. Maybe she should have brought her camera. He might even want some shots of the horses grazing on this beautiful fall morning. She continued walking, though not sure what Jack had in mind.

Shielding her eyes from the sun, she saw horses and beautiful landscaping, but no Jack. She waited under the shade of the old tree, wondering if she'd been mistaken.

Something caught her attention in the distance. A rider approached, and she knew it must be Jack. But he didn't look like Jack, certainly not the way she expected.

Jack galloped in her direction mounted upon Desert Wind. Kristi stood on her toes to get a better view, but as he grew closer, she saw he looked identical to a desert sheik. She held her breath at the sight of him. Against the green grass and clear azure sky, he rode clad in a royal blue, gold, and ivory woven robe. The sleeves folded up to reveal a white shirt and pants tied at the waist with a blue-and-gold twisted cord. A northern wind blew back the sides of a blue headpiece bound by a gold cord band. Golden coins hung over his brow, framing his face. Completely captivated, Kristi watched him swing over Desert Wind and step to the ground.

"You are magnificent," she breathed as he neared her. "I feel like I'm a part of *Arabian Nights*." Timidly, she reached out and touched his exquisite robe, then lifted her gaze to his beloved face. He smiled, and she caught sight of Desert Wind's full effect.

The same fabric as Jack's robe covered the horse's entire back. Blue braid trimmed the stallion's horse piece, and gold fringe hung below the flank. "And you," she murmured, patting Desert Wind's jeweled saddle, "rank second in splendor." The head costume boasted a royal blue bridle, and gold tassels dangled from the browband, throatlatch, and bit.

She turned back to the man standing beside her. "Jack, you are so handsome. What is the occasion? All of this. . ." She gestured to him and the stallion. "Why?"

He extended his hand, and she gladly gave hers to him. Slowly he bent to one knee, and kissed her hand. When his gray pools met hers, Kristi's heart suddenly began to hammer against her chest.

"Once I said you would look lovely seated upon Desert Wind dressed as an Arabian princess." She nodded, recalling his words. "I never forgot the look on your face that day, and I knew then I loved you. Now I'm asking you, Kristin Grace Franklin, to be my princess, my queen, and my wife."

Her hand flew to her mouth and she gasped. Never had she imagined what lay before her that day.

Barely above a whisper, he continued. "Only once in a man's life does God give him a woman to share his life." From inside his robe, he produced a small, black velvet box. Carefully opening it, he presented the diamond to her. "Will you be my wife, Kristi?"

She began to sob, and with trembling fingers she reached for the small box. She took in the glittering symbol of Jack's love, poised ready to encircle her finger. "Oh, yes," she breathed. "I. . .I love you with all my heart, and I will be your wife." She gazed into his face and back again at the ring. She felt the tears flowing from her eyes and over her cheeks. "Will you put it on for me?" she asked.

Jack rose from the ground and took the ring. He lifted it and slipped it onto her finger. His lips met hers in a silent pledge, kissing away her tears and promising his love for all of her tomorrows.

epilogue

"What are they doing out there?" Kristi asked while Cassidy studied Jack and Rand through the upstairs bedroom window.

"I don't know," the tiny blond replied. "Talking, I guess. Maybe Daddy is giving him some last minute advice about getting married."

"That makes sense. Don't know why I'm so nervous," Kristi stated, assessing her makeup in the mirror. She stood still. "Yes, I do. I'm getting married, and my stomach is fluttering like an army of butterflies. One hour from now, I will be Mrs. Jack Frazier."

Cassidy laughed, and Kristi turned to face the young woman. Her blue-gray eyes veiled in thick lashes seemed to fairly sparkle. The two women had become very close over the past three months since Rand had brought Cassidy to the bed and breakfast in mid-December. When Kristi couldn't decide whom to ask to be her maid of honor—with two stepsisters, two sister-in-laws, and a host of friends—she decided on Cassidy. The short-haired beauty had come a long way in her recovery from drugs, and her relationship with Jesus Christ deepened every day. Kristi had grown to treasure their friendship.

"I'm a mess," Kristi admitted. "I don't know whether to giggle or cry."

"You'll probably do both before the day is over," Cassidy replied. She glanced back outside. "Now your dad is joining them."

Kristi moved closer to the window. "I don't want Jack to

see me, but I'm curious as to what is going on in the yard."

"Hmm, maybe they are praying," the younger girl suggested. "Yes, I'm sure of it now."

"Good." Kristi breathed a sigh of relief. "I mean, I know he hasn't changed his mind."

Cassidy stood between her and the window. "You are a nervous wreck, and it's time to get into your dress."

"Okay." She took a quick glimpse at the clock on the dresser of the Victorian style bedroom. Giving an admiring glance at Cassidy, she thought how stunning the young girl looked in the floor-length red gown. "You are absolutely gorgeous," she said.

Cassidy turned to view herself in the mirror. "Must be my light coloring. Mom always likes the way I look in red." She flashed Kristi a smile. "Isn't it wonderful that she came with Daddy? I think she's really trying to put their marriage back together."

"I was watching them at the rehearsal dinner. It sure looked positive to me."

Cassidy pointed to the clock.

Kristi couldn't believe how the time had flown. "We have thirty minutes. Oh, my, and the photographer will want to take a few pictures before the ceremony. Quick, please help me into my dress."

Cassidy reached for the white wedding gown draped across the pale peach bedspread. "This is so beautiful," she murmured as Kristi stepped into it. Worn off the shoulders, the elegant gown featured a sculptured bodice and dropped waistline. Soft, pleated silk circled to the back where the full skirt drew up into an elegant, three-tier bustle.

"You take my breath away," Cassidy whispered once she'd fastened the gown. "And if I don't watch it, I'll be in tears."

"Don't you dare because we'll both ruin our makeup," Kristi warned, hastily blinking back any thought of emotion.

Her mother eased open the bedroom door and slipped inside. She'd chosen a mint green suit to wear for her daughter's wedding. It blended well with her hazel eyes, which began to swim at the sight of her daughter. "The most beautiful bride in the world," she claimed. "My little girl on her wedding day." Her shoulders lifted and fell. "I suppose your father is looking down from heaven and telling the angels the same thing."

"Oh, Mom, don't make me cry," Kristi pleaded. "This is supposed to be a happy occasion, and I'm already weepy."

"You're absolutely right," her mother said, taking a deep breath. "Let's get your veil in place before the photographer and Rick get here." She lifted the cathedral veil and positioned it perfectly. "I'm so glad you decided to wear your hair up and off your face. Don't you agree, Cassidy?"

"Definitely," the younger woman agreed. "Elegant, plus it makes her eyes look even larger."

A knock at the door brought Kristi's dad and the photographer. The camera flashed repeatedly: Kristi alone, Kristi with Cassidy, Kristi with her mother, Kristi with her dad, and more shots of Kristi with her mom and dad. At last he finished.

"I've got to go downstairs," her mother finally said. "I hear the music." She offered a brave smile and kissed Kristi's cheek. "I love you, sweetheart. This is the happiest day of your life. God bless you."

"Thank you, Mom," Kristi said. "And thanks for all you've done in helping me put this wedding together. I couldn't have done it without you."

Her mother smiled. She glanced up at her husband, and he brushed her lips with a kiss. "I'll be right beside you soon," he whispered as she reluctantly opened the door and disappeared. The soft sounds of the piano floated to Kristi's ears. She recognized "How Beautiful," a favorite song of hers and Jack's.

A moment later, Cassidy stood at the open door, carrying white roses woven with white satin ribbon. She heard her cue and turned to blow Kristi a kiss. "I love you," she whispered and stepped from the room.

"Are you ready, Baby Girl?" her dad asked.

Kristi nodded. "I'm so glad you, Mom, and I had prayer this morning. It has really helped me through these jitters."

"Good," he replied as she looped her arm into his.

"And thank you for being my dad and loving me," she continued.

"You're going to have me crying," he admitted.

"I'm not done yet. Remember the day you and Mom were married, and I cried all during the ceremony?" When he nodded, she continued. "It was the first time I ever really understood the meaning of love—ordained by God for a man and a woman. So thank you again. And I'm not saying another word, or I will lose it before I even see Jack."

He grinned. "Let's go then; it's our turn."

They began to descend the winding staircase adorned with satin bows and white silk flowers. "The Wedding March" echoed in her ears, and the crowd stood. Their friends smiled, and ladies dabbed their eyes. Rand gave her a thumbs-up sign and gathered up Lena's hand in his.

Then Kristi saw her groom. Smiling and teary, just like she. A piece of Scripture flashed across her mind. *"Delight yourself in the Lord and he will give you the desires of your heart."*

A Letter To Our

Dear Reader:

In order that we might better contribute enjoyment, we would appreciate your taking a respond to the following questions. We welcome yo and read each form and letter we receive. When comple return to the following:

Rebecca Germany, Fiction Editor
Heartsong Presents
PO Box 719
Uhrichsville, Ohio 44683

1. Did you enjoy reading *Equestrian Charm?*
   ☐ Very much. I would like to see more books
   by this author!
   ☐ Moderately
   I would have enjoyed it more if _____
   _____
   _____

2. Are you a member of **Heartsong Presents**? Yes ☐ No ☐
   If no, where did you purchase this book?_____
   _____

3. How would you rate, on a scale from 1 (poor) to 5 (superior),
   the cover design?_____

4. On a scale from 1 (poor) to 10 (superior), please rate the
   following elements.

   _____ Heroine   _____ Plot

   _____ Hero   _____ Inspirational theme

   _____ Setting   _____ Secondary characters

Readers

to your reading
few minutes to
ur comments
ted, please

because_____

_____

_____

e?_____

_____

_____

u like to see covered in future

sents books?_____

_____

_____

8. What are some inspirational themes you would like to see
   treated in future books?_____

   _____

   _____

9. Would you be interested in reading other **Heartsong
   Presents** titles?   Yes ❏   No ❏

10. Please check your age range:
    ❏ Under 18   ❏ 18-24   ❏ 25-34
    ❏ 35-45   ❏ 46-55   ❏ Over 55

11. How many hours per week do you read?_____

Name _____

Occupation _____

Address _____

City _____ State _____ Zip _____